TALON'S GRASP

Book I: The Demon and the Drowned Girl

by

Zachary Vaudo

and

Rebecca Eagle Lewis

Cover photography by Blake Griffin

ONE.

You ever get punched in the nuts by a dude possessed by a demon? Hurts like a bitch.

Now don't get me wrong: getting dinged in the dougan ain't exactly a pleasant thing to begin with, but with most guys I can take the hit. Throw a malicious, sadistic—and now pissed off—Babylonian shadow demon into the mix and it's like an express train right to the nads. Ain't exactly on my daily goal list, but here I am, out in the middle of the woods, getting mud in my boots, grass in my nose, and taking a haymaker to the love-maker via this Exorcist reject all because I couldn't just take my damn day off like a regular dude.

Let me back up a bit: folks call me Talon.

The world ain't as simple as you think it is. There is a world inside this one—living among this one. One filled with all the creatures that the media and your parents swore to you didn't really exist outside of stories. Amazing things, weird things, magickal things, terrifying things, all walking around under your very noses, with society none the wiser.

But you already knew that. You wouldn't have picked up this book if you didn't.

So you're sharing your world with a whole mess of creatures that go bump in the night. Me? I bump back, and I bump back hard. I work for a group called the Enclave down here in Georgia who employs folks like me to oversee the protection of this mortal coil. The Enclave is one group of shadowy cloaked old farts out of a whole slew that have formed up over time, either to address the same problem or to make it all worse. Different strokes, you know? I'm just glad I'm working down here and not someplace like New York or Chicago or L.A.: two or three times the population with sixty times the crazy. Pretty sure the world's nearly ended at least a dozen times in the last decade alone over in those parts. I'll take Atlanta any day of the week. Everyone's got their place in the world, and this one's mine. When something nasty puts a toe out of line down here, the Enclave calls me, and I go put a boot on that toe. And I've got a pretty fucking big boot.

I'm one of a handful of boots, too. The Enclave's got a whole platoon of people like me keeping the bad from hurting the good in this corner of the region. I mean, not *like me* (I'm way prettier), but doing the same thing as me: knocking heads and saving lives. Been doing this a long time—at least as long as I can remember, and I've gotten damn good at what I do. You could say I'm a bit of a household name in the supernatural circles around these parts, in good and bad ways.

It's a good gig: the Enclave puts me up with a pad off of Memorial and a damn decent income, and all I've got to do is go fight whatever asshole they point me towards whenever that asshole starts making normal folks' lives less than normal. All in a day's work. Fortunately for me, there's a whole lot of them out there, so things never get boring. There's enough of us in the mix that we split assignments, divide territories, sometimes even get days off—which is exactly what today was supposed to be, right up until I decided to screw that up.

I couldn't help it. I get bored easily when I've got nothing to do. It's not like I didn't try: I slept in, had a beer, did laundry, had another beer, cleaned my knife, tried to watch TV—normal stuff. Problem is, I'm not a normal-stuff kind of guy—least not for this long. Makes me restless, gets me itching for a walkabout and some action. If I wanted a boring routine of a day, I'd be an accountant, not a glorified supernatural bouncer. Besides, the longer I sit around and do nothing, the more I start to get lost in my own head, and that ain't a pretty place for anyone, much less myself. You let yourself bang around in your own mind with nothing to distract you, and you start kicking up memories of shit you tried to let go of a long time ago. Stuff you've seen that you can't forget. People you wanted to mean something in your life, but didn't. Or didn't have a chance to. Too much introspection will kill your buzz, so I gave my mind the finger and went looking for some trouble.

There wasn't anything on the Enclave radar, else they would've summoned me up by now (a day off's a purely nominal thing in this line of work...), which meant I had to go digging around on my own. When you're looking to stir up some action, you've got two choices: hit the bricks and see what you stumble across or go looking through less physical methods. In spite of my restlessness, I was feeling a bout of lazy on account of not doing much already—not to mention it was one of those patented freaking-hot days that we get so often, so I opted for not pounding the pavement.

There are a lot of perks to having a job like this, one of which being all the cool stuff you get your hands on, whether it's assigned to you, traded to you, or just found its way into your pockets after you pummeled the guy who was trying to use it against you. A guy can pull together a decent collection. The piece in question is an obsidian scrying mirror, about the size of my shoe and ink black. Scrying mirrors are pretty handy if you want to take a look at things happening around you connected to all things paranormal and weird. You don't have to be anyone special to use a scrying mirror: you just need to make sure you've got the real deal and not one of those New Age store knock-offs. Doing that involves a tiny ritual of clarity and giving the mirror a taste of what you're looking for. Trying to gaze into the past? Use dust and frame the ritual with your time period. Aiming to find a friend? Some of their hair will get things moving. Looking for love or sex? Well...

Since I was on the hunt for something nasty and violent, that meant the mirror needed blood. Blood's used for a lot of things, so how you draw it and apply it matters. A quick slit on my finger with my knife does the trick; that knife has seen the inside of too many bad things to count, so it's already got the taint of violence and evil on it. I flicked my blood onto the black mirror and watched the deep red splatters give the flat surface some texture. The blood soaked in as I recited the incantation, then started to swirl before forming a picture. The range on these things isn't so great—you need a bigger mirror and a stronger user to up your reach—so I was looking at maybe five miles in any direction, ten miles max. Luckily, you don't have to look all that far in the extended Atlanta area for some bad shit going down. The mirror shaped the blood into a view of the woods in Sweetwater Creek Park, and suddenly I had front-row seats to a young couple having a picnic by the lake.

At first I was confused. This couple didn't exactly look very intimidating or evil: just a dude and a chick eating lunch on a blanket, acting all lovey-dovey. Whole thing was like something out of one of those books where the folks on the cover are always almost kissing, but not quite yet. Except these two actually did start kissing and getting a little heavier than that. I didn't understand why the mirror was bringing me this; I felt more like a Peeping Tom than a protector. The couple kept going at it and the guy—Jacob, I found out later—started pulling at the girl's—Lorelei, I found out later—shirt. Now I ain't exactly a shy guy; I'll check out some tits if they're presented to me, but checking them out on a chick miles away who thought she was just having some private time with her boyfriend struck me the wrong way. My eyes fogged over as the mirror brought me into the scene, the couple's conversation echoing in my head.

The girl, Lorelei. "Not a bad way to spend our day off, if I may say so."

The guy, Jacob. "Yes you may. Are we ready for dessert?"

"I thought you'd never ask."

I figured the mirror caught my intention wrong, or maybe I wasn't in the right headspace to be doing this sort of thing. If your mind wanders during a ritual, you can find yourself all the way out in left field before you even realize you done fucked it up. I was just about to pack the mirror away and go Round 2 with the TV when the image shuddered a bit, and I saw it.

At first it just looked like a typical shadow, or as typical as a shadow can look when you're looking at one through a mirror coated in blood. Then I noticed the shadow was moving—no, *stalking*—through the grass, like a shapeless hunter bearing down on quarry. While the couple-next-door was busy exploring and getting lost in each other, the shadow reared up and showed me its ugly demon face. From the looks of it and the M.O., I guessed Babylonian or Assyrian, but there was no way to be certain or identify it further from the other side of this mirror. Before I had a chance to take a closer look, it threw itself effortlessly into Jacob's body. Lorelei didn't even notice the change. She just went on kissing and touching him. He did the same, right up until his hands found her throat.

"Babe, that's too hard." Poor girl was too caught up in the moment to tell rough sex from murderous intent, but she figured it out real quick when he tightened up instead of easing back. She grabbed uselessly at his wrists. "Jacob, stop!" But Jacob didn't say anything, and he didn't stop. He just grinned with devious determination.

When a demon possesses you, your body becomes its play thing. And demons play rough: they'll treat you like Play-Doh, Stretch Armstrong, and a Transformer all in one, bending and twisting and breaking your body however they see fit. You don't get to watch the whole time you're under, unless the demon's a particularly powerful and sadistic one, but the memories imprint on you during it all, so you get the recap at the end anyway…assuming you come out in one piece. The good news is that the demonic strength and healing factor means you recover quickly and only come out of it with a few bruises—assuming you come out of it. The bad news…well, you're possessed by a demon.

The demon took advantage of its body-warping abilities, stretching and elongating his fingers until they laced together around Lorelei's neck, crushing the life out of her. She went bug-eyed, gasping and trying to speak and hitting him with whatever minute strength she had next to the demon-power on top of her.

I threw the mirror down and bolted to my bike, hoping that the mirror was showing me the not-too-distant future instead of the present—or worse, the past. I knew the place, and if I broke a couple of traffic laws I could get there in a few minutes. Knife went into boot, coat went onto body, and body went onto bike as I sped off towards I-20.

And that's how I got myself in a position for a dick-kick from a demon.

TWO.

Sweetwater Creek Park's a nice place: lots of grass and places to hike, a huge reservoir that feeds into the creek, and loads of woods with places to get away from the general population, which is probably why the demon picked that spot to waylay victims. The park's mostly empty today despite how freaking beautiful it is outside, which means I can roll my bike through the parking area and up into the woods a bit without scaring any unwitting hikers and grillers.

I-20's a clusterfuck thanks to the most recent fallout between a local witch coven and gypsy clan, so I'm forced to take back roads, which screwed up any chance of a lead I had on the demon. Whole thing kicked off earlier this year: no one's rightly sure what started it, but the city's infrastructure has been feeling the effects of the curses and hexes getting lobbed back and forth ever since. I imagine I'll be called to step in at some point if things keep up like this: the Enclave has enough real-world excuses to cover for the current damages, but people are going to stop buying it eventually. But that'll come later, when I'm actually working; there are more pressing matters at hand.

I cut through dirt until the trees get too thick to ride, then hop off and tear a path toward the spot I saw on the mirror. The knife comes out of my boot the moment I dismount: I don't know if it'll do any damage to the demon, but I don't have my usual preparations, so the pigsticker'll do. My coat's slapping against tree trunks as I run, doing everything in its power to betray any semblance of stealth I may have. It's hard enough sneaking up on someone when you're as big as me. You'd think I'd ditch the noisy leather duster, but I love the damn thing too much to part with it. You know how hard it is to find something that fits me? I've already patched it up a half-dozen times. So I deal with its little quirks, including playing haka against my surroundings.

I plow through the brambles, listening for any signs of the couple. If I'd been a quicker thinker, I would have brought something to track them, so now I have to do it the old way of using my eyes and ears like some kind of savage. Good thing I know the area pretty well and was able to roll up to roughly the right spot because it's only another minute of running before I spot the clearing up ahead. Looks like the mirror gave me a glimpse at the future, which means I'm just barely in time.

Jacob's straddling Lorelei, pressing down on her like a half-empty toothpaste roll or some other overused cliché. Thanks to a little upgrade the Enclave gives to its employees, I can see the evil oozing off this guy from way back here. Poor dude: thought he was getting a nice day out with his girl, and now he's the newest ride for this demon prick. Through the thicket I can see Lorelei flailing, still fighting her impending death, but only barely at this point. No telling how much more life she's got in her from here, so I tense up on the knife and barrel ahead, measuring my distance to tackle the shadowy fucker.

I close in just as Lorelei's arm goes from flailing to lazy floundering and pull my knife back for a Caesar-style stab-in-the-back when the bastard whirls on me, quicker than I have a chance to react, and straight nails me in the nuts with his fist. In hindsight, I can't exactly blame him. I was coming up on him with a cheap shot myself, and he just happened to get the drop on me in response, but *goddamn* does it hurt getting belted below the belt!

The knife falls out of my grip as my hands instinctively go to cupping position, and the demon takes that opportunity to go for my eyes. The dude he's possessing already has kind of a weird face, the kind with long and wide proportions on everything, but the twisted demonic flair of being possessed makes the malevolent grin he throws on split his face near in two as he leaps off of Lorelei's body and flies at my face.

He lands on my chest, knocking my hat off my head, but it takes a lot more than a pissy Pazuzu wannabe to knock me over. My hands go from my crotch to demon-Jacob's arms as I stretch him out, keeping his vicious fingers from finding their way into my eyeballs. Demon-

Jacob struggles, spitting and cackling like a maniac trying to break free, until I can barely hang on to him. So I crucifix power-bomb the wormy fucker straight down into the dirt. It's a lot easier than holding him, plus it's good payback for the love tap. Demon-Jacob hits the ground spread-eagle and pops back up like a jack-in-the-box, right into my swinging boot. Boot meets face and Demon-Jacob goes airborne, somersaulting backwards on landing. Before he goes spring-loaded again, I'm on him with fists firing, doing my damnedest to punch the demon out of him.

My head goes sideways: the little shit's fighting dirty, yanking me around by the beard. I take the tug, throw my weight behind it, dropping all few-hundred pounds of big sexy on him, and start punching. Despite possessing the scrawniest guy he can find, the demon strength translates through the body. I only get a few hits in before he's got me by the wrists and flipping me over in one motion, going for my eyes again. I don't know what it is about demons and eyeballs, but if you ever square off with one, be sure to keep your hands up, else they'll reach over and rip them out as soon as they can.

"You picked the wrong day to play hero," the demon sneers at me, fingers wriggling toward my peepers.

"That's every day, dickhead." I grab his wrists with one hand and slap my other hand onto his face, fingers spread into the sign of my signature. The signature serves as an official decree of the Enclave, marking the demon as an enemy targeted for justice. Sort of a statement of "This is the police, put your hands on your head." It does double duty as a searing first strike to the demon. The gesture burns my calling card into the demon's brain just in time, sending him tumbling back, clawing at his head with an unholy shriek. I get just enough time to stagger back to my feet when he whirls on me, the shadows billowing up behind his host's eyes.

"Too late, Talon Pike," Demon-Jacob hisses. "Too late, too slow, too dead."

Demons aren't always the most creative in the word department—they prefer to show instead of tell, but he gets his point across. I finally realize I haven't checked on the girl since I ran in. I look down and see her stone still, eyes bugged out, her hair soaking up water from the creek. The demon takes advantage of the distraction and lunges for me once again, hopping onto my back and digging those spindly fingers into my shoulders. He wants me to scream from the pain. It sates him.

Fuck that, though. I grit my teeth and spin him around, trying to shake him. After half a minute of demon piggy-back, I tilt and drop straight back, crashing down on top of him. Not the most finessed of reactions, but it gets the job done. I feel a couple fingers snap before he yanks them out and freeing me. He reaches for me again, but I pop another one with some finesse before he can get a grip. Breaking things is an art, and I'm Picasso at it. Or at least Pollock.

I spin over and pin Demon-Jacob down with one arm. With a twist of my wrist and a quick whistle burst, the charm on the knife activates, pulling it back into my hand from its spot in the grass. Once it's returned to its rightful place, I push it up against Demon-

Jacob's throat.

"Yield," I grunt. Demon-Jacob giggles like an idiot, pushing up into the blade. A thin red line of Jacob's blood slips across the steel and trickles down the knife point.

"If you sliiiice," he sings at me, "it will be niiiice..." That hellfire grin nearly cracks Jacob's skull in half. "But it won't kill meeee...my soul it feeeeds..."

His rhyming shtick is stupid and juvenile, but I get the point: hurting Jacob won't hurt the demon inside. If anything, it'll make him happier. But that was never the plan. I just needed him to stop hopping around for five seconds.

"Feed on this," I throw out as I slap my hand on top of his face and start into the banishing.

There are a dozen ways to boot out evil spirits; every culture has its own methods, and a lot of them are really similar. Exorcisms, banishing rituals, cleansings. Some take a lot of time to set up, with props and designated space and all sorts of fanfare and floofy shit. My personal favorite is the Lesser Banishing Ritual of the Pentagram, good for cleaning an area of ill-intending energies. There's a reason so many different orders keep using it—the main reason being that it takes about thirty seconds to a minute to do it right. Even so, I've got one hand occupied trying to keep the demon from chowing down on my cheeks, so the ritual's going to be a little messy.

Keeping Demon-Jacob pinned down by the yapper, I mumble the opening chant. *"Ateh Malkuth ve-Geburah"* and so on. Soon as I'm done, I throw my other arm out behind me to make an awkward Qabalistic Cross, tracing a pentagram in the air with my knife hand and chanting out the Archangel Invocation, "Raphael before me, Gabriel behind me, May Michael be at my right hand, Uriel at my left..."

It's a rush job and I know it—I could be doing this a lot better and cleaner, but I'm not prepared enough to kill this demon right here and now. I just need to get him out of this body so he can't wreak any more havoc right now and I can get some more time to figure out what I'm up against, so sloppy and slapped-together it is. Eliphas Levi would be ashamed. Crowley'd get a kick out of it, though.

I drive the knife into the soil right above Demon-Jacob's head and dig into my coat pocket, hectically scrounging for any salt residue. Sure enough, my messy habits prove fruitful, and I get a few fingerfuls of Dead Sea salt from a previous job that has caked into the lining. Not enough to do much, but it'll help drive my point home. With visions of flaming pentagrams and six-rayed stars dancing in my head, I pull my hand off Demon-Jacob and throw the salt square in his face.

My hack job of the LBRP does the trick in a pinch: the demon's laughter turns to a howl as Jacob's veins pop black under his skin. The body quakes, the eyes go pitch, and then in a rush the blackness floods out and disperses, leaving just Jacob behind panting and sweating and shuddering. When a demon leaves your body, you get a weird withdrawal feeling, whether it's been in you for ten minutes or ten days. You get over it quickly, but it's expectedly unpleasant and gut-wrenching. And then there's the blood tears. Not full-blown Weeping Madonna or nothing, but the stress pops the blood vessels in the eyes and you hemorrhage just a bit to leak some life juice out. I'm just glad the banishing worked on such a short notice: I figured the archangels I was invoking would shake their high-and-mighty heads at my insolence and tell me to bless off. Lucky me.

I sit back and wipe the sweat off my forehead, shaking the dirt out of my hair—no small feat—before I pull the whole mane back into a tail. A quick once-over shows minimal damage: couple of scrapes and bruises, my shirt's got a nice rip across the midsection that shows off my gut and the little tattoo on my ribs. I ain't exactly one for a belly shirt, so I guess that's another top biting the dust.

I look around for my hat, but my eyes fall on the dead girl halfway into the water instead. The water is soaking through her white dress and her skin is already starting to pale, making the bruising around her neck pop out even worse. I can't see her face from this angle, but I'm going to have the frantic look of desperation that I saw through the mirror burned into my brain for the rest of the day.

No sign of His Royal Evilness: the woods are calm again, despite the trampled grass and a few broken branches. I don't have the right tools on me to track him, so I'll have to work on that one a bit. All that effort for nothing: couldn't kill the demon, couldn't save the girl. This one feels pretty personal compared to my usual assignments. At least this guy's not possessed anymore, but he's gonna have one hell of a freak out when he gets up.

Right on cue, Jacob groans as his eyes flicker open. It takes him exactly two seconds to realize where he is and what happened before the devastation sets in on his face and he starts crying hysterically.

"Oh God! Oh God, what did I do? What happened to me?" he screams, contorting on the ground. For half a moment I think he's possessed again and the demon's just fucking with me, he's kicking and twisting around so much, but a quick scan shows me that the

Babylonian bastard hightailed it out of here as far as possible once the ritual hit its high note. This is pure Jacob in pure agony.

"Just kill me," Jacob moans. "I don't deserve to live...oh God, what did I do? Lorelei? Lorelei?"

He's clawing at the ground, trying to get up. I stick a hand out and keep him in place—gently. Grief counseling isn't my strong suit, but I know well enough when to keep someone from going too far off the deep end. Physical contact snaps Jacob out of it enough to make eye contact. That's about the last thing I want to experience right now—a guy who just watched his body go for a spin without his control, killing his girlfriend—but it's too late now.

"Is...is she dead?" Jacob croaks, shivering. "Did I...?"

He doesn't understand. I can't blame him. Most normal folks can't grasp demonic possession in real life. They can barely handle the movies sometimes.

"This wasn't you," I offer slowly. "This was evil. A darkness took you over and forced you to kill the one closest to you. I tried to stop it, but I got here too late. Now it's gone and you're stuck with this."

Like I said: grief counseling isn't my strong suit. I pull a cigarette from my top coat pocket and dig around for a lighter. All my good ones are back home, but I find a shitty little Bic that's about halfway fueled and light up after a few false starts. Jacob looks at me stunned. Maybe I went a bit harder than I should have, but considering that I was trying to punch the demon out of his face a few minutes ago, I think I handled that succinctly and professionally. Finesse ain't exactly my strong suit. Hell, I have to look up how to spell it half the time.

Something feels funny. I tilt to the side and reach under my ass. There's my damn hat.

I need a drink. This is what I get for not taking my day off like a normal person.

"Wh...what?"

I exhale the smoke and watch it snake up over our heads.

"Yeah. Ain't that a bitch?"

THREE.

I move Lorelei's body into the water and walk Jacob out of the park before taking off. Jacob wanted to take her with him, but after a brief explanation as to the issues with carrying a dead girl around that you killed while possessed, he reluctantly saw my side of things. I would have loved to have given her a proper burial, but unfortunately this job makes me think of damage control first, feelings second. Once I'm sure Jacob's more or less sane and together, I swing back by my place to give my shirt a Viking funeral and swap it out for a new one. Then I steer my bike toward Rhys'.

Atlanta is a Frankenstein's Monster of a city, a patchwork of things that worked for other cities around the world, so Atlanta thought it could pull it off, too. New York has a big central city market? Atlanta gets one, too. London has a Ferris wheel? Boom, Atlanta gets one, too. If some other city has something cool, Atlanta will copy it and slam it down wherever it fits in an effort to appeal to the masses. This logic applies to the landscape of Atlanta—suburbs and parks and grassy fields side-by-side with modern cities and stretches of glass and asphalt—and it applies to the more-than-human landscape. Humans and nonhumans and inhumans and unhumans all living side-by-side, slapped together into a patchwork of life. The city has been stitched together raggedly and haphazardly in every way. Within twenty minutes I go from huge state park to Six Flags, through multiple suburbs to a pseudo college-town area and into the ratty area that houses Rhys' bar.

Rhys Eros runs one of the best places for those of the supernatural persuasion. An excellent hole-in-the-wall dive bar smack in the middle of the shitty part of downtown Atlanta, just outside of Old Fourth Ward. The perfect place for lowlifes like me. It's a good place to post up while I wait for the Enclave to call me in for an assignment. Or after I've just finished an assignment. Or on my way from the Enclave to an assignment. Or on a day off.

The bar's got a buttload of sigils and wards and runes and protective spells to dissuade the unwanted clientele, namely nosey fuckers and the Department of Health and Human Services. Rhys doesn't give a shit if you're human or otherwise: you're buying, he's serving. Some of the glamour on the place helps mask the real appearance of the creatures inside from the regular non-magick humans that stumble in, which is good, because I don't need some panicky mind-melting Average Joe shrieking his head off and ruining my beer.

All sorts frequent Rhys'. Demons, skinwalkers, vampires, magi, ghouls, you name it. Some come for the drinks and the atmosphere; others come for the other services Rhys has to offer. And damn, are they some fine-looking services. It works out well for the succubi and incubi: they get to feed their need and the customers get to feed their needs right back. Rhys is an incubus himself, so it's good rep for his species. He's a good guy, too: comps my drinks, throws me a freebie every now and again, always friendly when I come in on account of me bouncing a demon from his bar back when I first found the place. And because he knows I'll kick his ass otherwise, though I still do my fair share of bouncing when I'm hanging around, too. Mostly for my own amusement, but hey, if it benefits the group at large, I'll take the appreciation. Greater good and all that shit.

The guttural rumble of my engine bounces around the alley as I roll my bike in. My usual spot against the wall is free, so I walk my bike up and cut the engine, the grumble echoing off into silence. Does it say something about my drinking habits that the other patrons know to leave my spot open? Probably. I don't care right now: I just evicted a murdering shadow-demon from a grieving now-ex-boyfriend. I'll take my spot and take my drink.

The bar's at half capacity, as per usual, with more non-humans than humans, as per usual. There's a coven at a back table sharing nachos, still wearing their cloaks and the blood and ash smears across their faces from whatever ritual they just finished—Merry Beltane, ladies. A couple of vampires are eyeing their faces hungrily, but they control themselves and focus on their Extra-Bloody Marys (Rhys thinks the name's clever). The Damned's playing on the bar's stereo system—Rhys gave up on jukeboxes after the third time one of the recaps got into a fight with an alp and used it as a weapon. You ever squared off with an alp? Tiny little bastards, but those things'll jack you up if you let them. Keep them away from your nipples, though: they'll latch on like a hungry baby.

Even when he's telling you that black is white
Just some fancy dancing you can stop a fight
Grooving in the forest makes it all alright
What a man, a big hand
Neverland, Neverland

I pop a squat at the bar and Rhys walks up with a beer. Rhys is permanently stuck in the 1970s: slick-backed ponytail hair, big-collared shirts with a V deep enough to make sure I know his hair color is natural, pants too tight to give me any imagination—though in his defense, even my pants would probably give away the surprise. I can't see them from this angle, but I know he's wearing his saddle shoes with the half-platforms. You've got to appreciate a guy who picks what he likes and dedicates to it; dude's rocked it since it was in style and he'll rock it long after it's archaic. He nudges the beer into my hand.

"I assumed your usual, sir?" Rhys likes to call me "sir." It's his way of being sarcastic. I take the beer and toss back half of it.

"Never assume, Rhys. Makes an ass of you."

"...'And me?'"

"I already said that."

Rhys rolls his eyes. "How's your day off?"

"Anything but. Just took a roll in the hay with one of your cousins."

"You know not all demon-kind are related, right? We've been over that. Doesn't the Enclave put you through any kind of sensitivity training?"

"Are you saying I'm not in touch with your feelings? Because I'll touch them if you don't cut it out."

Rhys grins flirtatiously. "You couldn't

handle it."

"Not the kind of touch I meant." Rhys wasn't actually trying to flirt with me. He's a fluid kind of incubus, but I'm not up his alley and he's not up mine. Just in his nature.

"That bad, huh?"

I hit the beer again. "Don't wanna talk about it that much." I scan the bar. "She in?"

"Where else would I be," asks a voice over my shoulder, "if not right here?" I swivel on my stool and come face-to-forehead with a small, big-eyed woman. She's wearing a red leather jacket over her denim shirt, a litany of leather thongs around her neck adorned with various claws and teeth and trinkets. She smiles, her bright white teeth in sharp contrast to her dark skin and hair.

"Things going well, Talon?" She sits next to me, taking out her canvas sack as she does. Undoing the cord, she pulls out feathers, bones, and stones, laying them out on the bar in front of me.

"Things are bat-shit as usual, Crow, thanks for asking." Crow nods, continuing to empty her bag. Crow's a seer. She's Native American, but I don't know what tribe. I never asked and she never told me. At first I didn't care, then it felt awkward to just up and ask. Our relationship hasn't gone that way yet, staying limited to me buying her a beer and her giving me some guidance from time to time, whether I asked for it or not. I gave up fighting it and just roll with it now.

Crow keeps laying out the trinkets. This is our usual interaction: she pulls out pieces from the bag, and whatever's left inside somehow has to do with me. I don't get it and she doesn't explain it, but damn if it doesn't always help. It ain't exactly the end-all answer to my problems, but it's good to have a steer in the right direction. Rhys brings over her drink of choice.

"On the house as usual, big guy," he says to me. "Lemme know if you should be in need of anything else." He ambles back toward the other end of the bar to chat up some young nymph. Whether he's angling for business or himself, I can't hear. I take a long look around the bar again and shake my head at the number of unaware humans in here, sitting and drinking as if they're not two tables from a werewolf. Idiots probably can't figure out why it smells like wet dog in here. Any one of them could have been Lorelei earlier, not a clue in the world about this seedy underbelly and all the shit it brings with it.

"If all these humans knew," I muse. "They couldn't even handle it."

"It's for the best," Crow offers. "Many of them come to me for readings, a glimpse into a future they equally know nothing about. All this magick, all this glamour to make them see what they know to be familiar helps me to help them."

The werewolf is ogling the two hipsters on their third IPAs. They probably think that wet-dog smell is part of the charm of the place.

"Whole lotta weird here in my pleasure palace."

Crow shakes her head, letting her short hair fluff out a bit. "You gonna draw, Kubla Khan, or just survey your kingdom?"

The stereo changes over to Puscifer—I think Rhys changed it for me, he knows what I like—as I start sifting through the remaining items in Crow's bag.

Nature, nurture heaven and home
Sum of all, and by them, driven
To conquer every mountain shown
But I've never crossed the river

I pull out a small triangle stone, obsidian. It's got a funny mark on it: a little bird inside a diamond with some lines jutting out the top.

"The owl," Crow observes, "connected to darkness. A bad omen in this case. Departed souls. Watch out: there is much surrounding you that leads to danger."

Lorelei's cold, wet face pops into my head again and I sigh. "Could've used that a few hours ago."

"Choose another."

I fumble through the bag and wind up with a small chunk of limestone. A tiny bug's cut into the center.

"This is a group effort. The ant symbolizes teamwork. Choose again."

Angel, angel, what have I done?
I've faced the quakes, the wind, the fire
I've conquered country, crown, and throne
Why can't I cross this river?

The lyrics are catching my attention, and I try to push them out of my head and focus on the task at hand. I pull again, but my big ass fingers grab three instead of one. I go to drop a couple back in at random, but Crow grabs my hand before I can, shaking her head. She eases my fingers open and examines my choices.

"The noble and powerful elk helps with freedom...perhaps your angel friend? He has questions and answers for you. The bobcat...ah yes. I will set a meeting with her."

"Who?"

"In time. And lastly, the wise and studious crane. Your friend at the book store."

"Could've guessed that one."

"More answers through studies."

I put the stones down one by one into a triangle out of habit. "Well, once again, thanks for being ever so cryptic and elusive."

"I only offer a direction, not an instructional guide. All will come together in time, but for now I can only point you down the path." Her hands wrap around my hand.

I kill the rest of my beer and slide it towards Rhys' side of the bar, suppressing the urge to make an Indian Guide crack. Crow's not exactly a close personal friend, but she's shown me nothing but kindness, and I'm not about to let my assery ruin that just yet. "I guess I'll start with where I know and hit up the Library. Thanks, Crow."

When I take my hand back to leave, it taps her bag, knocking more pieces out. I pause and wait as they skitter along the bar top, bumping into the last ones I drew and knocking them out of their triangle: I may have gotten up to leave, but my hand "drew" the stones. So, unfortunately, these count. I huff a sigh and step back to the bar, giving a good look over the new arrivals.

A piece of bone with a slap of red. Some kind of tooth. A jet black slab with a something etched into it in gold: antlers? Hard to tell.

Lastly, a clear blue brick of a rock, detailed with sweeping white foam: water, waves, ocean? Inside the white and blue is a core of deep red.

Four more added to the pile.

When Crow doesn't respond, I move my eyes from the stones to her. She's perplexed, focused, silent. She's either wondering what these mean or wondering how they got into her bag. Or both. Eventually she speaks up, "I could tell you what these mean in their own right, but as for their relation now, I do not know. Their time for clarity has not come yet."

"That's it?"

"That's it."

"...huh."

"Come back tomorrow. I'll see what I can do about this one," she says, tapping the bobcat.

"Tomorrow it is. I'm gonna turn in and hit the Library before I see you."

I cross the bar and make for the exit, trying to put the lingering image of dead girls and mysterious stones out of my mind, hoping my next stop tomorrow proves a bit more

fruitful. Today's been a rough enough day as it
is.

It'll take a lot more than words and guns
A whole lot more than riches and muscle
The hands of the many must join as one
And together we'll cross the river

FOUR.

Ethan hikes through the woods, taking in the crisp late-afternoon air. He picked this part of the woods because it's nice and quiet, and most other hikers in this area stick to the trails further up. Over here, you can get to some really beautiful parts of the creek, away from everyone else. He pushes through the brush with his walking stick and keeps moving.

He stops. A small sound up ahead. Light, playful, pretty. What is it? He moves forward, trying to trace it. Ethan steps through the trees towards the creek and the sound grows a little louder. It sounds like singing. Wordless song and laughter. He rounds a large tree and there she is: a young woman in a clinging dress, lost in dance and song like she's the only one in the world. It's enthralling. She's breathtaking.

Ethan drops his walking stick, not focusing. She hears him and turns, brushing her slick wet hair back from her face. She giggles when she sees him, and Ethan's heart slams against his ribs. A lithe hand extends to him and he takes it, joining in her dance before he knows what's happening. There's no one else in the world but this beauty and he, lost in the dance.

She throws her head back and laughs, water flicking from the tips of her hair and running down the small of her back. He joins her. She sings in lyricless song, he tries to sing along. She spins him around, he trips and falls to the grass, laughing all the way. She lowers down to him, holding him and smiling. They kiss. Ethan is lost in her touch. Her breasts push through her soaked dress, and he takes them in his hands with joy. She kisses him deeper, deeper still.

Her head lifts up from his, smiling down at him as the water fills his lungs. He sputters and gags, trying to cough it out and take in air, but there's too much now. She smiles as he panics, smiles as the oxygen dies away and the serenity of drowning takes him over. Smiles as the life fades. Lorelei kisses his forehead and releases him to the waters. He floats down the way while she dances.

FIVE.

When you want to learn stuff, you go to the library. When I want to learn stuff, I go to the Library. The Library is an esoteric book store down behind Little Five Points, full of books and trinkets and items of magickal persuasion. Most people see it as a New Age shop, peddling books on the mysticism of nature and the Divine Spirit in all of us or some shit to willing saps. All that stuff's up near the front along with a bunch of geeky fandom crap to fund the place and keep said saps from exploring further back into the really interesting stuff. Underneath the stereotypical presentation, the Library is a point-of-information opened and monitored by the Enclave to give us enforcers an on-the-go port of resource if we need any advice on our runs. I come here more than the others, though, mostly because it lets me slack off a bit while still technically working.

    I told Crow I was going to stop in here yesterday, but I made an executive decision to go home and pass out instead, so I drop by on my way back to Rhys'. No calls from the Enclave just yet, so I'm officially extending my day off. They're lucky I don't bill them for yesterday, if we had a billing system for this kind of shit.

I walk in and go straight past the front section, ignoring the illusion of a salesperson crafted to help the unaware. If you're even the slightest bit aware of magick and charms, it's a pretty weak trick, but that goes to show you how many people don't pay attention to the folks helping them when they shop. Damn shame for the service industry, but it works in the Library's favor here. The illusion tries to greet me, but I'm already gone, into the rows of shelves, moving through the books on contemporary occult studies and republished grimoires. I hang a left and make my way to the back desk, towards the stacks of books and papers making sounds of consideration and approval. I stopped in front of the desk for a hot minute, not making a sound, before I let out a huge sniff and exhale.

"Ahhh, the Nerd Cave," I call out, the sound of dropped pens and surprise ringing out in response. "Find anything useful, Crayne?"

A head pops up from behind the stacks. Short brown hair not even close to styled on top of a round, bespectacled, and currently bewildered face: Abigail Marie Crayne, Library manager and Enclave resource. Crayne's a regular person, in a matter of speaking: not a shape-shifter or a mage or undead or otherplanely or any of that, which in effect makes her the most normal person I know. She's also one of the smartest people I know, spending damn near all her life studying and researching this crazy world of ours. She knows more than most of the books in this store—the ones up front and the ones back here—and she has enough of a collection to make up for the stuff she doesn't know yet. Our own personal supernatural encyclopedia.

I met Crayne around the time I met Rhys. Her brains helped me whip up an advantage to lay Big Horny out for the count and toss him from Rhys'. Since then, I got her hooked up with the Enclave, and now she's point of contact for the enforcers like me, though I'm the only one that'll strike up more than a two-minute conversation with her. What can I say, they're not all built like me.

Covering up for me startling her, Crayne resumed her reading as I walked up to her desk, pretending that she didn't just knock that cup full of pens on the floor. I'm sure they were just always there.

"All written word is useful. Knowledge is power, and power is useful," she responds to me, not looking up from her reading until the last few words, "is it not?" Flair for the dramatic, this one. It's accented by her Louisiana drawl; she's a transplant to Georgia by way of New Orleans, where she did most of her studying. Crayne likes to play the brains-over-brawn angle with me, mostly because we both get a kick out of it. Today I'm not in the mood for that kind of banter just yet.

"I wrapped up my day yesterday yanking a shadow demon out of a dude who strangled his girlfriend to death, so let me rephrase: anything useful to me right now?"

"Ah." Crayne adjusts her glasses—which I swear don't have real lenses in them, but I've never brought myself to call her on it—and spreads out a pile of newspapers next to her, opening up news websites on her computer at the same time. "Let's see what we've got." Crayne touches an amulet on her neck, muttering something under her breath to activate the four inlaid gems—a Descryer, one of the Enclave's many collected artifacts (I said she wasn't a mage, not that she didn't know what she was doing).

"There was something earlier..." The gems in the Descryer glow as she moves the pages around, trying to locate the useful ones. "Let me see..." I lean on the table as she keeps on sorting, until the Descryer finally glows blue and resonates.

"Aha! Here. I knew it was in one of the papers today." She pulls a page from the pile and forks it over to me, beaming all the while like she's showing me her straight-A report card; if it weren't all over a crazy killer demon, it'd be adorable.

"Thanks," I say, taking the paper. I scan the page until I find the headline:

LOCAL WOMAN FOUND BEATEN TO DEATH.

Authorities found the body of 27-year-old Stacy Kline yesterday in her Brookhaven home, bludgeoned to death. Police estimate time of death earlier in the day and are still searching for her husband, noted philanthropist Alec Kline, who has reportedly not been seen since before the incident. According to authorities, Kline is not a suspect and is presumed missing, but he may offer leads to the whereabouts of the killer.

Barely even warranted a quarter of a page and shitty ethics by the paper dropping names like that, but it works in our favor this time. Poor Stacy. If this is the same demon—and my bet's that it is, if the Descryer's pointing right to it—then that's two innocent women caught in the wake. "So my shadow demon's found himself another nice-guy face. Perfect. This won't be hard to fix at all."

Crayne taps further down the page. "There was another body found around the same time, apparently drowned. Not sure if it's related. Could be some idiot frat boys getting drunk and taking a nap in the water."

Following her hand, I read deeper. "Sweetwater Creek Park. Same place where I was. I'm thinking it's related."

"Your demon's leaving a trail. Tell me about it."

I squint, trying to remember. "It moved in the shadows, whatever shadows there were in the area. I guessed Babylonian or Assyrian from the face—had the same huge stupid grin as most of them."

"It's a decent guess. There's been a mild influx of activity related to Old World demons in the area recently."

"You don't say. Was this something the Enclave was going to tell me any time soon, or was this exercise just for funsies?"

"I imagine it was on their to-do list?"

"You know what was on my to-do list yesterday? Relax. Maybe do some laundry. Grab a few beers."

"That last one's not exactly a special feat."

"You know what wasn't on that list," I continue, ignoring her, "what wasn't even in the reserve pool of that list? Getting into a fistfight with a fucking shadow demon on my vacation. So since I'm already in this, do you have anything in your book of fix-its to remove this demon from this plane? Since apparently this is only news to me."

Crayne rolls her eyes and pulls up her laptop. "Calm your shit, Talon. It's somewhere in here." I suppress a grin as she searches. That's what I like about Crayne: never lets me give too much crap. She squints at the monitor as she rapid clicks and scrounges. "We haven't had any Babylonians on the radar yet, so I don't have anything on-hand you can use yet. May make things a little difficult."

"Any idea where it came from?"

"If it's Babylonian or Assyrian like you think? Just the afterlife."

"Oh, 'just' that."

"As in no special sculpture broken open, no summoning or evil ritual. Just an escaped spirit causing shit. And if it's NOT Babylonian or

Assyrian, then fuck if I know."

"Good enough, I guess."

She keeps searching for a few more minutes while I impatiently flip pages on a book next to me. Crayne pauses and looks at me sideways. "That books older than that ancient bike of yours. Quit touching it."

I put the book down. "Just got all riled up in the excitement of the wait."

"Clearly. Keep your hat on, I'm getting things together." Another minute of typing and she finally sits back. "So: had to throw some things together from the few Old World demons we've had recently and whatever research I had on demons from that part of the world. From what I can dig up, we're going to need candles—pink and red for the occasion—blessed sea salt, and...a bit of a Beast of Babylon."

I snort. "Well, I can see how the hardest part of that'll be the salt." Crayne resumes typing as I pinch between my eyes. I feel a headache coming on. "How exactly am I supposed to get a piece of a Beast that only comes around once every apocalypse? Do we just hop on eBay and see what we can find?"

"Actually...yes."

Wasn't expecting that. "Shut the fuck up."

"No, really."

"Seriously?"

"I can get a horn for twenty bucks if I bid in the next two minutes."

"No freaking way."

She spins the laptop, showing me the page. It's so simple, it's stupid: the thing's listed as a "replica fantasy paperweight." Whoever this is, they either have no idea what they've got or they're trying to get it off their hands as discretely as possible. There's a whole 'nother division of groups for illegal creature and artifact trade, but at the price this dude's asking, I'm going to go with the first option. "How do you even know it's the real thing?"

"Because," she starts, smiling triumphantly, "as I said before: knowledge is power. And I have the power." She expands the image on the screen and goes into lecture mode: "The Beast's horn doesn't grow like other horned animals, growing in a spiral pattern that starts inward and expands out. On top of that, this particular horn is adorned with all the markings and engravings that have been documented as part of rituals utilizing and celebrating the Beast." She jabs at her keyboard. "Done. Should be here by this evening: I sprung for express shipping."

"Aw, baby, you shouldn't have."

"I'm sure that I can fashion it into some kind of weapon you can use on the demon. All you have to do now is find him."

"Working on that. I need a beer."

"Go figure."

"What? It's a business meeting. Call me when you've got the thing situated and I'll come grab it."

"Naturally." She waves me away as she opens up her books again, picking up wherever she left off when I arrived. I make my way back towards the front door; it's just about time to meet Crow and her mysterious bobcat. So far this day's gone pretty well.

Which probably means it's gonna suck by the end of it.

SIX.

With Crayne deep into the mystical world of online bidding, I make my way back to Rhys' to meet up with Crow and her bobcat.

Even at this time of day the bar's still got customers. There aren't a whole lot of places where everyone in the more-than-normal world can gather up without a fuss, so business stays pretty steady. I roll in and go to park, but my usual spot's blocked by some P.O.S. Jeep I've never seen before. Must be one of the "normal" customers. Rhys got some Enclave-approved magicks going to bring them in, coupled with the usual glamour so they don't know they're sitting right next to things that can eat them or worse. I let it slide—normies don't know me typically, so they don't know that I've got my preferences that I like to keep to—but now I'm already in a pissy mood as I have to park my bike way in the back like some goddamn creature of the night. I swear, if one of those undead motherfuckers that lurk back here knocks over my bike, I can't be held responsible for my actions.

I push the door open, letting some twangy guitar riff spill out into the open air. I take a quick scan the room for the most likely candidate to own that junk heap in my spot so I can educate them in their mistaken ways—I changed my mind on letting it slide between the parking lot and here. My mission is interrupted when my eyes land on a well-dressed and radiant man at the bar. I don't mean radiant in an admiring-him kind of way, I mean honest-to-gods glowing around the edges, as angels tend to do. I can never tell if it's a completely natural thing or if they do it to show off. Plenty of angels hide among humans from time to time and they're not always glowing, so it's just a question of whether they're putting in the effort to hide the glow or if they're putting in the effort SPECIFICALLY to glow when they're in tangible human form. I never asked, though; it'd be rude of me.

Oh yeah, by the way: angels exist. This one here's called Taniel, and he's about the only one I've met that I can stand. Taniel's an archangel—not an Archangel, not one of the Big

Seven, just one of the tier. Unlike the rest of his tier, he spends a lot of time shutting back and forth between Heaven and Earth, mostly because he's on a sort of probation for trying to help humans a bit more directly than the system likes. That's probably why I like him over any of the other ones I've met. They've all got personalities of their own, but the detached-from-life thing gets in my craw a bit. Taniel's alright by me, he helps me however he can while still sticking within the guidelines of his probation, which I appreciate. I don't want to cost him his livelihood, or whatever the word would be for angel jobs.

Now you may be asking yourself: if angels and demons are real, that must mean that Heaven and Hell are real, so how can you do all this magick stuff that's not in the Bible? Well, glad you asked: just because one thing's real doesn't mean the rest of it isn't real either. All that One True crap gets played out by the humans who follow whatever path they're on, but look closely and far enough back, and you'll see that all these folks have been begrudgingly acknowledging the existence of everything else for a long time. Yeah, not following the path of the angels may mean I don't wind up in Heaven at the end of it, but honestly? I don't want to hang out with most of those guys anyway. There are a lot of options for guys like me outside the binary Heaven-Hell options; I'm sure one of those'll be fun. Maybe I'll be a ghost. That'd be awesome: keep doing what I'm doing with 100% less pesky flesh and bone.

Taniel nods at me as I walk up to the bar. Rhys slides a beer my way and keeps on walking—he and Taniel don't exactly see eye-to-eye, but he lets him in the bar on account of me. As I take a seat and pull from the beer, Taniel clears his throat—for show, of course. "I had a feeling I would find you here. What did you need from me?"

"How did you—?" I catch myself from asking the dumb question; I still forget about the angelic mind games from time to time. "Never mind, I don't want to know." Which is a lie, but it helps me save face for a bit. "I need you to put a lo-jack on this dude," I continue, pulling out a picture I found of Alec Kline at Crayne's. "There's a real good chance he's possessed by a shadow demon, one I tangled with not too long ago. I want to find him and vanquish his ass before this gets any more out of hand."

Taniel chuckles. "To address your first question—" Damn, I was hoping he'd given up on that. "—I know what I need to know. Knowledge is power, right?"

Did everyone get the same fortune cookie today?

"And as to your request," he continues, "I will do what I can to track him down for you. I am, of course, under certain limitations."

"Usual angel red tape. Got it."

"ARCHangel," he emphasizes, a little curtly. I know how to get under his skin, same way he knows how to get under mine.

"Archangel *on probation*," I clarify for him.

He sighs dismissively, feigning indifference. "When you return I will have your answers concerning this one. For now, I believe you are awaited." He points over my shoulder. I turn and see Crow at her table, with someone sitting next to her. I swig the beer again and turn back, but Taniel's already gone.

"Thanks?...I hate it when he does that."

"You're telling me," Rhys chimes in, walking back over.

"Yeah, but you hate him anyway."

Rhys shrugs, neither confirming nor denying.

"They been over there long?"

"All day."

"Well, time to meet the bobcat, I guess."

Rhys gives me a look. "Crow stuff," I explain. He shakes his head and goes back to bartending as I hop off the stool and make my way over. As I get closer to the table, I finally see who sitting next to Crow. She's decked out like she belongs in the Carpathians hunting old-time monsters: high boots with a wicked blade tucked in each, hide straps, leather pants—*real* leather, none of that shiny shit. Her face is mostly hidden by the crazy length of dark hair, but as she talks to Crow I see sharp and stern facial features, ones that don't screw around when there's business to be done. Bobcat was a good description: she looks like she could take a guy my size down if they rubbed her the wrong way, so naturally I want to make a good first impression. I do that by sitting right down at their table while they're talking and planting my beer in front of me.

"What's good, Crow?"

Crow smiles. This new woman glares at me, sizing me up. Before she makes any kind of decision, Crow introduces me. "Talon Pike, this is my friend Catarina. I spoke of her to you earlier. She has information that I believe you will find invaluable."

Catarina gives me a look like she'd rather play Seven Minutes in Heaven with the Golgathan than share information with me; I pretend not to notice, but let's be honest, that hurts my feelings a little, y'know? I've barely even said two sentences yet and this chick thinks she's already got a bead on me. Talk about judging a book by its cover—and I'm a damn good-looking cover, too, which means this one's got no taste in fine literature. She looks to Crow for reassurance, and Crow—thankfully—steps up to bat for me: "He's a good man, Catarina. You can trust him."

Still reluctantly, Catarina pulls a very modern tablet out of her very ancient-looking satchel and boots it up. Placing it in front of me, she swipes around some articles, all reports on drowning victims along Sweetwater Creek. One of them rings a bell: the article Crayne pulled up for me earlier. "This one," I stop her, dropping my finger on the tablet screen. "I saw this one earlier. Are these related to the shadow demon?"

Catarina shakes her head, sending her hair in distracting waves, and finally does me the honor of speaking to me. "This is an indirect result of our shadow demon, Talon Pike." Her voice matches the Eastern European look, with a hint of some other region of the world. If I had to take a guess, I'd throw in for gypsy. She continues: "I have heard that your dealings with the shadow demon happened along these waters, where a young woman was murdered. She is the one responsible for these deaths."

"How? She's a corpse," I ask gruffly,

trying to act like I'm still not thinking about her. "We buried her in the river."

"And that is how," Catarina replies disdainfully. "She is rusalka, a woman taken before her time, killed violently by the water. Poor girl," she sighs, "she never had a chance." I bite my tongue to let her continue. "My people have experience with these poor souls. I must find her and plead with her to stop, before more innocents are killed. Her murder must be avenged."

I take a long, slow draw off my beer, trying to take this in. Now, not only do I have to deal with not being able to save this girl from an asshole demon I'm trying to hunt down, my not being able to save her turned her into a wrathful water ghost. My vacation just gets better and better. I should tell Catarina to go handle it and try to put it out of my head. Better yet, I should tell the Enclave about all of this and let them assign people to sort it out. But I don't do either of those things.

"I'll go back and speak to her. This was my problem; I can handle this little lady myself.

No need placing you in harm's way."

The fire that wells up in Catarina's eyes tells me that I've definitely picked the wrong option. Not even sure why I threw in that last part: emphasis, maybe? Either way, the table's not on my side. Crow shakes her head as Catarina's face knots up. She cocks her head down and spits at the floor near me. "You think me incapable? I should curse you for the insult you give to me, to my people. Crow, this man is useless to me: *I* shall help this poor girl *myself*."

Catarina stands up while Crow lays a hand on her arm, trying to steady her. I laugh. I can't help it. I shouldn't be laughing. I've obviously pissed her off, and my reaction's not helping to calm that at all, but you know how you can't help but laugh when you know something that someone else doesn't? Curse me...please. As if she's the first woman to try, much less the first anything. I learned my lesson on magick words a long time ago: I'm decked out in so much anti-hoodoo and spell-be-gone that it'd take a blessing by a full witchy chorus line through the Horn of Gondor to curse me. So even though I feel bad about pissing Catarina off, I can't stop my laugh, which only infuriates her more. She glares at me as I drink more.

"You couldn't curse me if you tried," I start, but Crow cuts in.

"The both of you: calm yourselves! Talon, Catarina is Romani." Score one for me. "And her heritage is as strong as it is ancient. Believe me when I say: if she wishes to curse you, it will be done. None of your tricks could stop it, and neither could I. You were told this would be a group effort, so you must work together on this. Remember?"

"I remember," I say, and for a change of pace I let it be with that. If Crow thinks Catarina can take me on, there might actually be something to it, so I might as well hear this out.

"And Catarina," Crow continues, "you must trust him. He may be brusque, but he is of The Enclave. He fights for the protection of the people, and he does have others' best interests at heart, especially in this matter."

Catarina looks at me, sharing the same look of defeat I'm sporting, and sits back down.

"As you wish. But know this: cross me, and I wear your balls as a trophy."

I changed my mind. I like her already.

She reaches into one of her other pouches and produces an even smaller leather pouch, tied together with a thin strip. I take it as she tosses it to me. "What's this?"

"Your basic mojo bag for protection. Alligator teeth, amethyst, herbs and oils. You may be guarded, but you will need it to protect you from the rusalka's charms so that she may not entrance you while we speak with her."

I turn the bag over in my hand. It stinks to high heaven, and I'm hoping Rhys doesn't decide to kick me out for the offending odor. But as far as my limited knowledge in this arena goes, it looks like it's on the level. I give another look at Catarina, a hard look. She's ready for action, but it's backed by a pity for Lorelei and what she's become. She's ready to cut down anything in her way except for her: she truly wants her to rest in peace, not rest in pieces.

She's good by me. I finish my beer and stand. "Well, darlin': your ride or mine?"

SEVEN.

Go figure: it was Catarina's Jeep in my spot. I bite my tongue as we get in and she pulls out, the clunker rocking on its wheels like it was built to bobble. My bike's old, but it's that classic kind of old; this thing's just dirt-old. We leave Rhys' in a cloud of exhaust and I vow silently that next ride, we skip the Shitmobile and take my bike. The trip's a taciturn one: Catarina doesn't say much (you'd almost think she doesn't like me or something), and my brain's on the demon instead of the task at hand. I should have killed it when I had the chance, but I was in a rush and underestimated it. If I'd taken a minute to think it over instead of Galahading straight into the fray, I could have grabbed something from my place that could've done more damage to the demon. What, exactly, I didn't know, but surely there's something in the mass of tools and tricks I've taken from various ne'er-do-wells that could pack more of a punch than my own punches.

It was stupid and careless and it let the demon go hurt more people. I should've gone to kill. Better yet, I should've been on the clock or called it in to the Enclave. They might have had someone closer to the area. I put that fleeting thought out of my head in an instant: I've rarely, if ever, been the one to call in for backup if I could, in any way at all, handle it myself. And that was most of the time. Still, given where we sit, that may have been one of those rare-if-evers that could have made a world of difference for Lorelei—a lifetime of difference, even.

I drop those thoughts out of my head for the moment. Internalized self-loathing is a hobby of mine, but so's vengeance against wrongdoers, so I pick the more constructive of the two and focus on the tasks at hand. We're already en route to Lorelei, so while I wait for arrival, I pull out my phone and dial up Crayne to check on our mail-to-order Horn of Babylon. She picks up after a few rings.

"Weapon arrive yet, Crayne?"

"It's not a weapon yet. Right now, it's a very rare yet insanely inexpensive artifact, only one of perhaps a dozen or so left in existence."

I roll my eyes and Catarina casts a

perplexed glance at my dramatics. I rephrase: "Very rare artifact that we're gonna turn into a weapon arrive yet?"

"It says the package is on the way, but it's not here yet."

"Kinda running on a deadline."

"I told you 'this evening.' Tracking says by 8 p.m."

I groan loudly enough that it startles Catarina, and I hold up an apologetic hand. "I'm feeling a little vulnerable without it, buddy," I start, pulling my hand back and rubbing it down my face in aggravation. "Could really use a better turnaround time."

"Take it up with the post office," Crayne retorts, not having any of my shit. Then, a little more helpfully, "You'll be the first to know once it gets here, friend. Let me handle it."

"Alright, keep me posted. I'm on my way to talk to a drowned girl."

"What now?"

"Tell you about it later."

I hang up and drop the phone back into my coat pocket. Looking over to the driver's seat,

Catarina is trading attention between the road and me, confused and curious. "Trouble at the office?" she asks teasingly, the first hint of light-heartedness I've gotten out of her. There's hope for her yet.

"Special delivery for the shadow demon's taking a little longer than I'd like. We'll swing by later tonight; it should be there by then."

She nods quietly, but her face says that she's still not fully clear on it. Fine by me—keeps a bit of mystery in the air. Speaking of the air, the bag around my neck is starting to burn my nostrils. All the oils and herbs cooking in the leather pouch against my chest are brewing up one nasty cocktail of smells.

"Man, this mojo bag stinks," I grumble. I look over to Catarina for support and notice her neck looking awfully bare and devoid of leather pouches. "Hey...why don't you have one?"

Catarina laughs, one of amusement and condescendence. "Many reasons. I am a woman, for one. As her death was at the hands of a man, possessed or not, she will have no interest in harming females."

"Seems a little biased."

"It is the nature of her demise. The event is seared into her mind, shaping her form and purpose beyond the grave. I am no threat to her; therefore I am not subject to her charms and spells. And furthermore: I am protected by birthright, as are all of my people."

"Lucky you. I guess I'm like a Happy Meal to her without the protection, then?"

"To say the least." She shifts gears, physically with the car as well as conversationally. "So, this 'special delivery' is a weapon, you say?"

"Yeah. Just a little something I need to rid us of that shadow demon once and for all."

"For one of this strength, you would need a piece of the beast of Babylon for this..." Her voice trails off as I grin. Her eyes widen in surprise, and it's my turn to laugh. "You found it? Where?!"

"I have a powerful and knowledgeable friend. And don't say 'knowledge is power' or I'll pull the wheel from you."

She looks at me, perplexed and somewhat awed. I let the mood hold for a minute before I throw her a bone. "Nah, I'm kidding, it was on eBay." That just makes her even more confused. "Besides, if she were that powerful of a friend, we'd have had one-hour delivery."

We drive on for a ways more until we reach the park. Catarina glides—a word I use generously—her Jeep into a parking space, and we enter the woods toward the scene of the crime. They hadn't closed the whole park down fortunately, but some caution tape had been haphazardly slapped up along with a brand new sign to let attendees know that the area "may be dangerous." Could've used one of those the other day, guys. I knock the tape down unceremoniously and push onwards. Catarina flashes me another look of disappointment—that's going to get old fast—and follows behind as we close in on the creek. My hand slides up to the mojo bag, making sure it didn't slip off or come loose.

A few more yards and we're there, feet

on the bank of the creek where Lorelei died. I stand there for a minute, waiting for Catarina to do her thing and bring Lorelei around. After a while, I turn to her and notice that she's standing there waiting, just the same as me.

"I thought you knew how to talk to her."

"I do," she replies, "but not until she shows herself."

"I thought you knew how to do that, too."

"Aren't *you* the monster hunter and finder?"

"Don't even act like those knives in your boots are for whittling. Besides, those things tend to run the other direction when I come around."

"Full of yourself as usual. I should have never let Crow convince me to bring you along."

"Honey, like I said back at Rhys': this is my problem, so I'm along for the ride the whole way."

"Why you—"

Catarina is cut off by a light giggle. We stop dead in the middle of arguing, not moving a muscle. Eventually, the giggling is replaced by a soft lull of song. I turn around with Catarina. Now, many of the creatures I've encountered make their way through daily human life thanks to a healthy dose of illusion—glamour. It helps them pass more among the Man on the Street. Thanks to the constant charms that are always in effect, I can cut through the glamour and see right down into the true nature and form of what I'm dealing with. For once, I wish that wasn't the case.

I thought I'd be dealing with Lorelei, but I was wrong. She's not Lorelei. Not anymore. Whatever was left of Lorelei has been replaced by vengeance in a shell of what remains of her. Her eyes, the bright eyes that I watched go dim and dead at the hands of her puppeteered boyfriend, are now covered by glamour, to give those not in the know the sense that they were still there; those of us in the know, however, could see the emptiness, the sucking vortices that lead down into the pit of whatever substituted for a soul in this body.

Her smile on the glamoured surface

looks sweet and caring and inviting, but underneath it all it's carved into her face like a wicked Jack-O-Lantern's constant grin. Her soft and small hands have nasty hooks and barbs at the tips: the better to snare you with, my dear. She's soaking wet, hair matted down into a flat black plank along her head, her already-sheer white dress pressed against her body, slick and see-through, taunting and teasing the unsuspecting victims she would exact her vengeance upon. This is not the poor girl I couldn't save. This is the monster that stepped into her body and soul, holding it on this mortal coil and twisting it while it took up residence. For one of the few times in my life, I relaxed the charms and let myself see her for what she projected, though flickers of the truth still danced underneath—you can't truly shut it off once you turn it on.

Lorelei—no, the *rusalka*—gives me a warm, endearing smile and reaches toward me, inviting me to join her, play with her, become one with her in the water...but before she can reach me, she stops and shivers. Her eyes, the dead eyes beneath the illusions, lock onto to Catarina's mojo bag. It looks like Catarina's old magick is working just fine: the rusalka realizes she can't reach me with her usual bag of tricks, and that pisses her off something fierce. She shakes and starts a scream mixed with pain, anger, and betrayal that pierces through the protection of the bag and my own arsenal. I clap my hands over my ears to shield myself from the sound, but Catarina looks entirely unfazed by the whole experience. She steps forward, addressing the rusalka directly and delicately. "Beautiful one, we wish to avenge your death."

"Beautiful one" my ass, but the rusalka stops screaming for a moment to take in Catarina's offer, which is long enough for me to uncover my ears. I have to resist the urge to put her down, remembering that despite what she's become, she still is Lorelei somewhere in there, and what's left of Lorelei can never be free so long as this creature takes her place.

Catarina keeps going. "Let us find the one who did this to you—the REAL one who did this—and end his terror. Allow us the chance to grant you peace."

The rusalka considers this briefly, the blank eyes locked onto Catarina. She—it—scans back to me before reaching her decision. Her voice dances like dragonflies on water, though the split-faced mouth never moves: "You have until the next setting of the sun to avenge me...or I shall continue to drown my pain." With that she tips backwards and falls into the creek, vanishing below the surface as she hits, gone in a splash.

I watch the waters for a while as the ripples fade, taking the shell of Lorelei with them. "A day and a quarter to find the demon and bring it down. No pressure."

"We will make do with what we have been given," Catarina says.

"So you're hunting this demon with me, now?"

"This demon has brought sorrow and suffering to the final moments of this poor girl. I will do what I must to aide in its demise."

"I don't mean to rain on your parade, but *I* had trouble with this thing. I appreciate the extra hands, but I don't know how much good it'll be."

"I will do what I must," she repeats, and I accept it for what it's worth, but I don't show it.

"Well...fine. I hope this works."

"It must," Catarina responds. "There is no other way...unless we banish her soul to a demon realm."

"I don't think I could feel comfortable with that, even after seeing what she's become."

A low hiss interrupts us, starting from behind us and filling the area all around us as it grows.

"Yesssss. Pleease. A new playmate for all of our friends would be sssssoooo welcome......"

I know that voice. It has a slightly different sound to it now, but that's what happens when you hop bodies. Underneath that, it's the same sinister voice that taunted me right up until I forced it out of Lorelei's boyfriend. I turn on my heel, Catarina a moment behind, to face the demonically possessed Alec Kline.

"And we are alwaysss in need of new toysss...."

EIGHT.

Alec Kline—the man from the news article, wanted for questioning in the savage murder of his wife—now stands before us on the river bank. Underneath Alec's skin is the shadowy demon that sent Lorelei to her watery demise. He's seeping wisps of darkness like a sieve, the trails that haven't faded yet spindling and tapering back to the darker patches of the forest, marking his path of approach all the way to us. Like Lorelei, his grin sprawls backwards and up his face as far as he can, but it's not hidden under glamour here: thanks to the wonders of demonic possession, that's Alec's actual grin stretched beyond human constrictions. Demons love to pull that contortion shit, bastardizing the human body; I experienced it with demon-Jacob and his crazy extending fingers earlier, and now demon-Alec was giving me a show of it with his Halloween-mask smile. I don't even acknowledge it.

"You're in major violation of way too many things to even list. Leave this man's body in peace and I'll only hurt you a little bit."

Catarina sidles up next to me. "You do not have the horn," she whispers hurriedly.

"Not a whole lotta time to worry about that," I hiss back quickly. The shadow demon starts up again.

"But we don't wish to leave." I hate when demons do that "we" shit, acting like every single one of them is Legion or something. It's seriously worn out. "There are sssstill so many bodies to explore. Still so many bodiessss to leave behind...." Demon-Alec cackles with glee at his little joke. I've had just about enough, horn or no horn.

"I'll give you a damn body," I toss back, and I throw mine at him as a follow-up.

Now, as I may have already mentioned to you: I'm a pretty big guy. Most folks don't have much on me, and I tend to rival some of the bigger baddies I square off with, so needless to say the last place I expect to wind up in this situation is on my back a handful of feet away after demon-Alec grabs me in mid-run and tosses me like a dog playing with a chew toy. But

that's exactly where I land, with a resounding
thud to compliment my new position.

Before I can even process it, he's right
over me again, his grin unbreaking in spite of his
face, his voice like an engine full of glass. "New
play things are always a treat…"

For the next few moments, I'm a rag doll
in his hands. It's a sensation I'm not used to,
being utterly manhandled like this. I once tried
to bounce a gargoyle from Rhys'—apparently the
correct term would be "grotesque," since
gargoyles are the ones with the water spouts
running through their necks, making it hard for
them to get up and move around…or so Crayne
made a point to tell me, but no one except art
snobs and historians make the distinction
nowadays. Though to be fair: the way this dude
pounded back drinks, you'd think he had a water
drain running through him. He was a squat little
dude who'd pull up roots from Oakland
Cemetery every few nights to get stone cold
hammered—pun only partially intended. No
one's quite sure how he got animated in the first
place; we think the dude who's buried in his spot

may have been a mage or had some ties with the community, and Rocko (I don't know his real name, I just called him that because he's made of rocks, and I'm not all that original) is just the by-product of that magickal leaking. Or maybe he was there specifically to guard the dude's grave. Either way, the result is a semi-living statue with a drinking problem. He got a little unruly one night and broke a table in half trying to sit on it, so I tried to do Rhys a favor and bounce him out. Fucker picked me straight up in the air one-handed in return. It was surprising, to say the least.

Point is: getting knocked around in a fight is one thing, but it's an occasion to mark when I actually get tossed around like it's not even a thing.

This is unfortunately such an occasion. Demon-Alec treats me like a child's play thing, throwing me from grassy patch to rotting tree trunk to muddy spot along the river. I don't even have a chance to get my bearings before I'm being grabbed and tossed to the next spot. It's without a doubt the most annoying fight I've ever been in. I swing my fists wildly when I feel his hands on me again, too disoriented to line up a proper punch, and I connect with glancing blows, but I still go flying again and again. *Where the hell is Catarina in all of this?* I ask myself as the bastard bears down on me once again. I can't take another flight.

Right on cue, he lurches forward, one of Catarina's boot-knives sticking out of his shoulder. She thinks she's hurt him from where she's standing, but from my angle I can see that he's more irritated than anything. Catarina cocks her arm back and sends her second knife flying. This one doesn't meet its mark, stopping in his clenched fist. Blood trickles down from Alec's hand, but the demon inside him doesn't seem to notice, squeezing down harder to taunt Catarina. Her hand thrusts into one of her pouches. "Talon!" she calls to me, throwing something in a high arc over Alec toward me. Focusing at just the last moment, I reach up and catch it: a small, silver flask. I'm betting this isn't meant for me, as kind of a gesture as it would be, so I spin the lid until it flies off to the side and chuck the contents without question right in demon-Alec's face as he turns back to me.

The holy water does the trick: the demon shrieks a miserable cry as Alec clutches his sizzling face, stumbling back and giving me space. That gives me enough time to rise to my feet and get level again. I didn't come prepare to fight the demon; I had been expecting Taniel to get a line on it first, so I don't have anything useful on me. I should take a cue from Catarina and get one of those leather satchels. Keeping a grab bag of goodies on me might come in handy. For now, though, I go the usual route of Talon's Special Fisticuffs, twisting the couple of rings to warm up the enchantments engraved in them. I got the idea from a movie, but the Enclave vetoed me having brass knuckles—a huge bit of unfair profiling if you ask me—and opted instead for the rings they already had in archive. They help me pack an extra special punch when the occasion calls for it, but they burn out quick and take forever to warm back up again, so I try not to use them too much. Right now, though, I can use the boost.

I have to remind myself as I hit Alec Kline in the face repeatedly that this isn't really Alec at the moment. The demon will heal his wounds rapidly to maintain the worth of its possession, and when I finally kick the son of a bitch out, there's a solid chance Alec might not even remember the beating he took. The rings glow brighter with each hit I land, feeding off the momentum, drawing small scars on Alec's cheeks that cut beneath the surface, down to the demon layer. Spindles of shadow curl out of the cuts as the demon takes the damage, but it's only holding him at bay. These rings are general-use, not designed with any particular creature in mind, so it's only a matter of time before demon-Alec strikes back.

The demon lets me get a few more shots in before he grabs on and hammer-throws me right into Catarina. I do my best to roll my weight on impact so I don't give her the full brunt of the blow, but we both go down hard. I'm going to need a frequent flier plan if I get thrown around anymore today. I go to check on Catarina, but she's already getting up and going for another weapon. She pulls yet another knife—I'll have to ask where she keeps those—but it gets kicked from her hand by demon-Alec just as soon as she gets a grip on it. He looms over us, boxing us in.

"No more play," he rumbles, skin rippling as the demon inside pushes and contorts his body. I see the fingers starting to stretch into claws, the gums recede ever so slightly to give length to teeth. "Time to tear you to ribbons." The grin, by some sinister means, grows even wider, and I'm afraid Alec's head is going to crack in half from the strain. "Splice and slice," he sing-songs, "inch by inch, strip by strip, and then on to the next—"

Alec's grandstanding is interrupted by a hammer to the face.

He stumbles and snarls, minus a tooth from the blow, as the owner of the hammer steps between him and us. From the ground we get a good view of a pair of vinyl-covered boots, old-school and beat to shit. The boots support a punk little prick decked out in a zipper-covered jacket, ripped jeans, a half dozen wards, and one of the most annoyingly smug faces I've seen: my fellow Enclave enforcer, Corbin Beck. Corbin's wielding his modified one-handed sledgehammer, decked out with Qabbalistic symbols and Hebrew inscriptions to give it added force, the majority of which recently went into the shadow demon's ever-moving mouth. Corbin wastes no time stepping up to bat for a few more swings at the demon, going full John Henry on him.

The hammer rings out with a high pitched **_TING!_** at every hit, deceptively light against the force of the impact. Corbin gets three or four good swings in before demon-Alec has enough and gets a hand around Corbin's throat, hurling him back into me as I get to my feet, forcing me to catch the bastard out of instinct. With Corbin's body blocking my view, I lose sight of Alec, but I hear his voice hiss out:

"You don't play fair..."

Crybaby. Before I can drop Corbin and clear my line of sight, Alec's gone. That's two for two on letting this bastard go instead of finishing him off. I'm starting to lose my edge, which is making me lose my cool. If I don't get my hands on that Horn soon, I'll lose him yet again and our promise to the rusalka will be null and void. Today's shaping up to be a pretty shit day.

I brush myself off and feel my fingers catch. I look down and see yet another shirt reduced to ribbons, courtesy of the demon. "Fuuuuuuuuuuuuck." This is not my week for fashion.

Corbin gets up, dusting off his jacket and jeans—I never said I dropped him gracefully. "Nice bloody work, Talon," he sneers in that annoyingly British accent. I've always suspected he's putting it on for show. There's no way one person can be THAT much of a stereotype.

"Me?" I throw back. "You didn't exactly nail him down yourself."

He passes his hammer back and forth from hand to hand impatiently, dissatisfied that he didn't get to use it enough. I examine my hat: smeared with mud, naturally. I slap the thing against my leg trying to clean it off while Corbin saunters forward and starts lecturing.

"Do you even know what you just got thrown around by? That was an *udug*, sometimes called an *utukku*. Very popular demon that springs up to spread havoc and dismay wherever it can. This area right here is the fourth instance of possession. The *utukku* takes a host, causes all kinds of pain and suffering, then it leaves when it breaks the host beyond personal enjoyment. Somehow this one got into our city a week ago and starting raising a heinous mess."

There's so much hot air I'm sweating, but Corbin's not done yet. "The Enclave assigned me to the demon, which you'd know if you paid the least amount of attention to anything but your own bleeding self. I found out that it took out a girl here and figured he'd come back to gloat over his last kill." I hold in a smug smile of my own. I should tell him what I know—*should*—but watching Corbin be wrong is sort of a hobby of mine. He narrows his eyes at me. "I was prepping my trap when you lumbered in and sent the whole thing to shit!"

"No one gave me a notice."

He points at me with that damned hammer, the gold-inlayed Star of David on the top of the hammer head lined up under my nose. I can see the energy built up in the core of the hammer cooling down from use. "I'm your goddamn notice, Talon. This one's *mine*. I've got this."

"Sure looks like you do, Corbin."

The hammer twitches in front of me before he pulls it back and leans it on his shoulder. "You've been informed. Steer clear." With that, he turns on one heel and storms off. I stare a hole in his back as he exits. The nerve of this guy, right? I ought to nail his ass to the wall with that damn Fischer-Price hammer. I give my hat a few more slaps for good measure and put it back on, wincing as it hits the wrong part of my leg. I feel a bruise forming. Hell, I feel them forming all over my damn body: my face probably looks like someone played jazz drums on it.

Catarina walks up beside me while I'm in the middle of rage-glaring at Corbin's retreating back. From the corner of my eye I can see that she's even more confused than before. *Stick with me, kid, and you'll never understand what's going on.*

"And...who exactly was *that*," she eventually asks.

My phone starts buzzing before I come up with a sarcastic enough answer to capture my mood. I push her flask back into her hands as I answer the phone. "Disgruntled co-worker," I mutter, by way of a response. "What?"

"Nice to hear you, too." Crayne's drawl spills through the phone. "Your package has arrived."

I breathe a sigh of relief. "Perfect timing." Not really. Could've used it about three minutes ago, but it's as perfect of timing as I can ask for under the circumstances. "Thanks, Crayne. Keep the shop open: we're on our way." I kill the line and pocket the phone, looking down at my pants in the process. Covered in mud and soaked down one side, with more holes in them than usual. Damn shame. I really liked this pair. Sacrificed to a good cause, at least.

I turn to Catarina. "Crayne's got the

Horn. Mind if we stop by my place first? Can't go saving the city from a bloodthirsty demon with my cod swingin' around. Sends the wrong message."

"By all means, spare me and the rest of society the horror." She resheaths her knives in her boots one at a time and starts the hike back to her Jeep, with me in tow. "If you're going to free the world of evil, you should at least do it in something other than a belly shirt."

"Maybe there's time for another beer after I grab my new weapon," I offer, hearing a barely-audible snort from her as she goes. Catarina passes through the tree line; I pause before I follow, turning back to the open area and the creek.

The rusalka's gone, but I can feel her lingering presence, even with the protection of Catarina's mojo bag, which has somehow survived the fight with only a couple of dents. Moreover, I can feel Lorelei's presence underneath the rusalka. Facing down what she's become, it was hard to feel, but without the horror in front of me overshadowing everything, the feeling is stronger. Her soul is still tied to this area, waiting to be freed from the personal hell this *utukku* crafted for her with her boyfriend's unwilling hands.

I'll free you, Lorelei. I'll free you and I'll finish this.

That shadowy bastard's going down.

NINE.

Catarina waits outside while I change. I invited her in, but she opted against it, saying something about "den of degeneracy," whatever that means. So much for my gentlemanly manners.

I change quickly and clean the scratch marks off my gut. Demon-Alec got some good ones in on me, but at least he didn't fuck up my ink. Once that's all tidied up, I grab some general supplies for the road: chalk, more salt, an extra lighter, a couple vials of holy water (inspired by Catarina), and a Sharpie (you never know when you need one). I stuff them all in my pockets before hopping back into Catarina's Jeep and heading over to the Library. We only have to stop and restart the Jeep once this ride, which Catarina remarks is an improvement.

The Library's closed to the public, but Crayne's kept it "open" for me. Holding my hand like a spear, I put my fingers to the door to cut through the spell-supported lock and twist my wrist, turning my hand into the key that opens the lock. It's a remedial technique, but thanks to the Enclave it only works for Enforcers and other related agents. Folks not on the guest list get to stand there looking like idiots doing the first steps of the Macarena at a closed door.

The door pops open and I usher Catarina in before closing the door behind me. We move to the back of the shop, where Crayne's still ever-immersed in research, either for other Enforcers or her own personal enjoyment. Never met a girl who gets off on history and books like her. I'm not saying I'm anti-education or nothing, but the things I've met in real-life are enough for me; I don't need to learn about all the shit that already happened when history's repeating itself nice and conveniently for me already. I walk up and rap-tap-tap on the edge of Crayne's desk to bring her out of Study World, but she's still digging through the desk drawers and piles on the floor. Red swirled candles litter the top of the desk.

"Hang on," she says absently, "I left it around here somewhere."

"Well while you're looking: Crayne, this is Catarina. Catarina: meet Crayne."

"Hello," Catarina says, a hell of a lot friendlier a greeting than she gave me. "You are Talon's weapon-making friend?"

Crayne's still digging around and starts answering Catarina dismissively—until she looks up and takes a good look at her. "Yes, that's me..." Crayne's voice catches when she lays eyes on Catarina, and she instinctively straightens her blazer and fixes her hair. "...as well as being a great well of knowledge for our mutual friend here. Catarina...the name and your facial features tell me Romani, yes?"

She's laying on the Cajun accent thick, and I try to hold a straight face. I can't remember the last time I saw Crayne try to flirt with someone. It's almost adorable, in a geeky kinda way. I bite my tongue and let her throw the charm for a bit.

Catarina smiles warmly. "Yes, and also a great source of knowledge, I am told." I swear if someone drops the "knowledge is power" line again, leaving."

"I can tell," Crayne says, damn near purring. I'll have to break this up at some point, but it's too damn amusing for now. "The Romani people have a long tradition of mystic brilliance, dating back to old India."

"You know your history," Catarina muses.

"I know many things," Crayne says, leaning her elbows on the table. "Feel free to pick my brain."

That's enough of that. I drop a trigger in the conversation to break it up. "Yeah, Crayne knows lots of stuff. Ask her about the crawfish."

Crayne's flirtatious airs break at the word and she points a wary finger in my direction. "I'll be able to prove that in time, now. It's all right there, just a matter of getting the last connections. You'll see." Crayne has an uncharacteristic prejudice against crawfish for a Cajun. Thinks they're the last Earthly remnants of the Old Gods or something. It's become an obsessive side-project for her that's all too convenient to bring up when I want to tease her or undercut her attempt at being suave around whomever she's got her eye on, like right now.

Everyone's got their trigger-points. Remember that.

"Nasty demon-spawn," she mutters under her breath while Catarina stifles a laugh, looking to me for an explanation. Crayne narrows her eyes as she finally looks in my direction. "Talon, you look like microwaved hell."

"Yeah, thanks for noticing. Had a little run-in with our demon after we got off the phone. Would've been a lot easier if I had my Horn..."

"I'll leave a shipping review." Crayne shakes her head, forgetting her flirtation and resuming her search for the Horn. "You made it out alright, though. I take it the demon's still on the loose?"

"Yeah, Corbin showed up and gave it a few whacks before bitching that I was stepping on his job. It got away."

"He hasn't come to me for any help, so I didn't know he was on it, too." Crayne smirks as she keeps digging. "He still playing at Judah

Maccabee, then?" Crayne had a little schoolgirl crush on Corbin when she joined up in this role, until she realized what we already knew about his charming personality. "One of these days he'll get a—AHA!" Crayne cuts herself off, producing the modified Horn weapon from under the table. "Right where I left it."

She's fashioned the Horn into a wicked looking dagger, breaking the pale white Horn up into sections and fixing them into some kind of cut-quartz blade. The engravings of the Horn still show up on the outside; she may have even cleaned them up a bit, making them stand out stronger. The blade's wrapped in a thin gold band, winding its way down to the blue leather handle. "I've affixed the pieces here and here," she gestures, showing it off. "I also rubbed blessed sea salt from the Dead Sea into the blade and handle. It's active and ready to go."

"Is it as simple as I think it is?" I ask, taking the dagger by the hilt.

"Just about," Crayne grins. "Once you find the possessed Mr. Kline, you'll need to stab him full force—" she gestures enthusiastically, nearly throwing herself into the desk "—to wriggle the demon from the host."

"That sounds an awful lot like it'll kill him, Crayne."

"Hopefully not."

"Hopefully?"

"Well the Assyrians and Babylonians weren't always partial to saving the ones possessed by demons. And seeing how you didn't give me enough information to figure out what *kind* it was—"

"*Utukku*," I interrupt. "Corbin called it that. Or *udug*."

Crayne's face stays stoic for a bit, processing, then she walks away from the desk and into one of the back rooms. Catarina and I stand there waiting.

Catarina turns to me. "She made a weapon without knowing what she was up against?"

"She did the best with what I gave her."

"Why did she not go to this Enclave and ask for details?"

"Because, as Corbin so enthusiastically

pointed out, it's not my assignment. If she went to them, they'd funnel her to whoever was in charge with her research."

"What does that matter? Her knowledge would help him defeat this demon, with or without you. Are you so selfish that you feel you must shoulder this burden entirely yourself?"

"*Yes*," I snap back. "Yes I do. I was the one who saw Lorelei dying. Not you, not Corbin, not anyone else. I was the one who saw it, I was the one who went there, I was the one who couldn't save her. So yeah, I feel a bit of a personal responsibility to the matter. Can you blame me?"

Catarina wants to be right—I know that look in her eyes—but she restrains herself. "I suppose I cannot."

"Besides, I'm not by myself. You're here at Crayne's with me, right?"

Before she can respond, Crayne reemerges, cradling a jar of red liquid, deeper than the candles. She reaches her hand out and I hand her the dagger. Popping the top off, Crayne dips the dagger in blade first, holding it there for a while before pulling it back out and handing it to me. "Don't ask," she says, interrupting me before I have a chance to, "but it'll be more useful now that I know what we're dealing with. You're lucky I even had this."

"You had something specifically for *utukku* killing?"

"No. Yes. Sort of. Can I get back to telling you how to do this without killing Alec Kline?"

"You *don't* want to explain everything to me in terms I don't understand? Who are you and where's Crayne?"

"Hah hah, jackass. Fine: Corbin's only half right. It's an *utukku*, but the wicked and vengeful type, which very technically makes it an *edimmu*."

"I take it back, you can stop."

She didn't. "The *edimmu* are demons created in a variety of ways, but the most common way is improper burial—most likely due to the nature of their lives and deaths. So I've soaked the blade in a solution for that: embalming fluid."

"And what if that wasn't the way this one was formed?"

"This isn't a perfect weapon, Talon. This is as close to one as we can get, but there are variables. Just hope this does the trick. Now: back to not killing Alec. The way this is set up, the blade should act as a mystic hook, snaring and pulling the demon out. Just be careful where you strike."

I nod, processing about half of what she told me. Catarina looks impressed. "Embalming fluid as a symbolic representation of proper burial. Brilliant improvisation."

Crayne starts to grin, and I see the nerd-seduction wheels turning, but I don't have time for that again. "Right, don't kill the guy. No problem. What about the candles?"

I watch the excitement change gears from attraction to research. "Ah, yes, I was getting to that. Basic banishing. Set the candles up in a pentacle." She scoops the candles into a bag and hands them to Catarina with care. "After you hook the demon, you'll have control of him for only a few moments. They're wily little shits.

Drag him into the center of the candle set-up, and you'll hold him longer. Banish him...or beat the hell out of him at that point. Your call, but whichever works faster."

"I'll probably do both. Probably throw a Seal of Solomon down on top of it, too, to be safe. He's a wriggly fucker, and the LBRP just kinda pissed him off. I'll keep you posted." I waggle the dagger. "Thanks, Crayne."

Catarina finishes examining the candles and closes the bag. She gives a warm smile. "It was very nice to meet you. Good luck on your...crawfish, was it?"

Crayne mumbles something in the way of a goodbye and buries herself back in her stacks of books as we exit and steer ourselves back to Rhys' bar.

TEN.

A few of the bar patrons get nervous when we walk in, and it takes me a moment to realize that they probably feel the dagger resonating in my coat. I'd forgotten that the Horn has weird effects on a lot of creatures, and some of them are starting to feel funny in its presence, modified as it is. I try my best to give a reassuring "this-isn't-for-you" look to the ones giving me the side-eye, and it quells the tensions (or puts them off enough to stop looking at me and pretend that things are normal). I spy Crow in her usual spot at the same time Catarina does.

"I must converse with Crow," she tells me, following it up with a stern look. "Tell me when your friend has located this demon." I give a nod as Catarina walks off, taking the bag of candles from her to consolidate inventory. I watch her take her seat, then scan the bar for Taniel. He's back in the same spot I found him before, a beer already awaiting me. It's nice to be expected.

I take a load off and start drinking.

"Well, Mrs. Fredric, I see you have returned."

Taniel gives me the mildest of irritated looks. "I have told you time and time again, Talon: I have no knowledge or use for your 'pop culture' references." I grin a big ol' shit-eating grin. That's exactly why I do them. It's been a private game of mine to see how far removed I can go with Taniel. Despite his high-and-mighty statement, he's tried to catch on to my references, but I just go more niche each time. Poor fucker only just got my Castiel reference last time before I switched it up to *Warehouse 13* now. I'm barely even trying at this point.

The grin stays plastered on my face as I drink again. "Did you track down our demon?"

"I did," he nods. "He should be in the alleyway behind this bar soon."

I just about choke on my beer at that one. "*Here?*" That wasn't exactly the plan. "Did he follow me here, or did you think it'd be easier to find him if you sent him an angelic evite?"

"I only traced him, as you requested."

"Then what? Is he looking for a new host? This is the wrong neighborhood for that."

"It is possible. However," Taniel says plainly, "I believe he followed this one, who followed you." He gestures lazily behind me, and I turn around.

Jacob Rocca stands right behind my stool. He's barely holding himself together, minute spasms sparking across his face as he stands with his arms nearly wrapped around his torso, making an attempt to contain the shakes. His forehead's got that clammy look which tells me he's been sweating and wiping it off just as fast as it beads up. That thousand-yard-stare I left him with is still tucked away behind his eyes, but it's been replaced with something new, and my jaw almost drops as I piece it together.

It's Awareness I'm seeing in there. Not your usual cognizant awareness, but an understanding that he's not in a normal place, a peering through the glamour kind of awareness. That wasn't there when I found him, which means this is new. This is left over from evicting the *utukku* or *edimmu* or whatever the fuck we're calling it now. Jacob looks at me like he's ready to bolt as soon as possible.

"Hi," he manages.

"You're seeing," I muster back, and I can tell he knows what I mean.

"Yeah."

"...the demon?"

Jacob barely nods. "I think so. It happened after you left. I finally got to walk home and I just kept walking until I hit Piedmont Park."

"That's a hell of a walk."

He nods emptily. "I slept overnight on Ponce. Behind the Majestic. I realized where I was, looked around to get my bearings, and I nearly shit my pants when I saw some kind of demon cat in the bushes."

My turn to nod, sympathetic. "Tailypo. She hangs around that area." That's a hell of a thing to start your new sight with, personally speaking.

"I ran into Little Five and thought I was going crazy," he continues. It's not that far off, I imagine, at least from a regular person's perspective. "I kept seeing all kinds of crazy shit the more I walked around, and I didn't know why. I think some of that darkness stayed in me...makes me see all this stuff." He clears his throat and calms his tremors, which picked up while he talked. "I wandered away as fast I could, trying to get away from everything, and I kept walking further and further way until I got here and saw your bike parked out here. I came in here to find you, and the guy at the bar said you were out. I've been sitting here waiting for you to get back for hours, trying to pretend like I'm not seeing what I'm seeing all around me."

"You are," I say unhelpfully. "Sorry to break it to you. To my understanding, these demons usually leave of their own volition when their host is all good and broken. I kicked him out of you against his will, which means he didn't have time to get his shit in order, and it looks like you got stuck with a piece of him."

Jacob's mouth opens and closes like he's running out of air. "I...I don't want this."

Man, this was not on my list of things to do today. "I'm sorry, but you've got it now. No real way around it. This is the really real world around you, Jacob. The one you were pleasantly ignorant to until just about twenty-four hours ago. There's no going back." Jacob looks like he's going to cry, but I can't let up until he understands. "And to make matters worse, the darkness—the demon that possessed you—is on his way here. Possibly for me, possibly for you."

Now Jacob looks like he'll piss himself. "Here," he croaks, "now?"

I nod. "So you need to get out of here as fast as possible."

"I can't," he quakes. "I can't face this. I need your help. I don't know what to do out there, not like this. And not if that thing is going to chase me all over again."

Shit. This *seriously* was not on my list of things to do. I need to be prepping the area for our surprise demon guest that I wasn't expecting so soon and now I've got to get Jacob the hell out of here and deal with him another time. My head hurts, and I realize that I haven't had a cigarette since the exorcism. Fuck it: I'm empty, and this is as good a time to quit as any, I suppose. I can't be focusing on cravings when I need to resolve all of this, *now*.

Taniel, who's been entirely too quiet this whole time, shuffles his feet and leans forward. "He is but a few minutes away. Time is of the essence, Talon, if you are to have the advantage."

It finally dawns on me. "You don't want to leave, Jacob? You want my help? Fine. I need your help." He looks at me like I'm the crazy one. "Yeah, you, help. You had this demon in your head, which gives us a certain advantage if you can dig it up: I need the demon's name."

Jacob shakes his head. "I don't remem—" he starts, but I cut him off.

"Yes, you do. It's buried deep in there, along with whatever's left of him. You don't know it's there, but it is. Possession isn't necessarily a one-way street. Demons can be symbiotic when they need to keep the host going for a while, just like he was planning with you and like he's doing with his current host. Dig deep, find the name, and we have a better chance of smiting his ass once and for all."

I tense as Jacob eyes the door, contemplating running away. If he runs, we've still got the dagger, but I can use all the upper hands I can get right now. I've heard every name for this demon except its real one and having that can make all the difference. Despite the ambient noise of the bar, our area seems dead quiet, save for the music leaking in from above us:

Someday Someday I'll wake to be myself again
(But) I left my soul and I Never want to try again
Never want to try again
I left my soul and I Never want to try again

After a minute of eternity, Jacob slowly nods. "Okay. I can do this. I think I can do this." I nod with approval. If I were in his shoes, I'd have seriously considered running as well. But I can tell he wants to do right by Lorelei, even though he can't bring himself to say her name.

"You can do this," I agree.

Taniel tenses. "He is almost here."

I rise from my barstool. "Let me get Catarina and we can—"

Before I can finish, it's Taniel's turn to cut me off, placing one hand on me and another on Jacob.

"Innocents are in danger. We must hurry."

And before I can protest, all three of us are in the alley behind Rhys' in a flash of white light. Neat trick: I've never traveled by angel before. Jacob sounds like he's going to hurl from the trip, though.

"Easy," I say, extending an arm to him. "It's never comfortable." I take a look around the alley: wet, dank, and dark. Perfect for the demon: there's about a million shadows to escape into if he wants, which means I can't give him the opportunity. Catarina's gonna kill me that she didn't come along, but that's the way the pendulum swings, as the Enclave puts it.

There's probably a less-ominous sounding way to put that.

I sling the bag of candles into Taniel's arms along with my chalk. "Seal of Solomon with the chalk, pentacle with the candles. Light 'em up when he shows."

"I'll do what I can," Taniel says flatly, already starting the circle of the Seal.

"Jacob, I hate to do this to you, but you'll need to stand just in front of the Seal. He'll come for you, but when you announce his name it'll throw him off-guard enough for me to do my thing with barely any resistance."

"You want me in his path?" Jacob looks like he's regretting this decision. I nod.

"It's the best way. He'll be focused on you more than the Seal, which means he's more likely to get close."

"I still don't remember what his name is!"

I sigh. "It's alright: it'll come to you." Jacob still looks worried. "Look: you being here will still lure him in. If he gets too close and you haven't remembered his name yet, I'll blindside him."

I hear a noise and whirl around, expecting to find Alec Kline ready to pounce. Instead I see one of the bar vamps making out with one of Rhys' girls. The last thing we need is an audience—or snacks for Alec. I bellow at them: "Leave this place!" They jump and take off running, looking for more private quarters. I guess the rooms upstairs were taken, or the vamp's a cheapskate. I turn back to Jacob. "Be brave." Then I throw in the cheap shot: "Do it for Lorelei."

That cinches it. He clenches his jaw, dangerously close to breaking some teeth, and plants himself in front of Taniel's Seal. I duck behind a corner and draw the dagger, laying in wait. Any minute now.

From the other end of the alley, a ghastly voice echoes.

"I...sssssmell.....a sweeeeeeeet...treeeeeeeeeeat..."

"Any minute" is over. The demon Alec Kline is here.

ELEVEN.

You ever see in the movies when the supernatural bad guy enters the room and the whole scene darkens? They stopped doing it eventually—someone in Hollywood probably thought it looked cheesy. That someone never stood in the same area as a pissed-off Babylonian shadow demon. I could feel the air getting heavier as Alec Kline stepped into the alleyway.

Demons and angels tend not to get along well, and the *utukku* in Alec could probably smell Taniel in the air, so he was pulling out all the stops. "A nice sweet treat for me," his voice seeped through the alleyway, "I smell an angel with no wings...all the power I shall have..."

"Not if I have anything to say about it," I mutter. I look up at Jacob, who's trembling ferociously but standing his ground as best as he can. I've got to hand it to him: going from zero to a hundred in the span of a day is no easy feat, but he's doing the best he can to honor Lorelei, and that deserves some respect. Now I just have to hope I can get this demon nice and dead so all this is worthwhile. Jacob's eyes race back and forth as he looks for the demon, and I can almost see the gears grinding in his head as he tries to remember the damned thing's name. I'm hoping he comes up with it fast.

Alec steps into view, way down at the far end of the alley. He looks worse than before: the demon seems to be coursing through his veins at this point, popping them black and bold beneath the skin like it did with Jacob on our first encounter. Unlike Jacob, Alec's face looks harrowed and bony, like the life is slowly draining out from him through those wisps of shadow still wicking off Alec's body. The shadows curl down the alley, reaching forward, groping for anything living in their path. Every step he takes forward is jerky and erratic: the demon's turned him into a broken marionette of a man. I hug the corner, trying to see everything while staying out of sight, hoping that sense of smell he bragged about is metaphorical and he can't actually catch a whiff of me.

Demon-Alec actually looks surprised

when he lays evil eyes on Jacob. "A special surprise snack," he gurgles. "Did you miss us, Jacob Rocca?" Jacob nearly bolts, but he locks his knees and stands rigid. The demon's so focused on Jacob that I'm betting he hasn't noticed Taniel making the Seal just behind the dumpster a foot or two from Jacob's back—not only do I bet that, I'm banking on it heavily.

Jacob's voice is bathed in fear, cracking and quaking, but he speaks up to the demon nonetheless: "I'm here to stop you."

A horrible sound bounces off the wall, and it takes me a hot minute to realize that Alec is laughing. "Come to stop ussss?" The damn hissing again. Does he think he's not creepy enough or something? "Can't stop us like this. Couldn't stop us from squeeeeeeezing the life from precious Lorelei..." Jacob rocks, the words a knife to the heart. The demon doesn't let up. "Couldn't stop us from *crushing* her like the insect you humans are...you're going to stop us now?" That bark of a laugh cuts through the alley again.

I need to get things rolling now, and

fast, before Jacob loses his nerve. I turn toward Taniel and the Seal. "We almost ready?"

Taniel is standing in the center of the Seal. It's masterfully crafted, the lines bold and white, intersecting with each other seamlessly. The five candles are placed to form a perfectly spaced pentacle laid on top of the Seal. It's all set and ready to be activated so it can contain the demon-Alec. And Taniel's there in the middle, holding the lighter in his hand, lit up and burning steadily. He looks up at me helplessly.

"Taniel?"

"I'm sorry..."

Taniel extends the lighter toward one of the candles, and I see his arm slow down as it nears the wick, almost as if he's moving through mud. He gets slower and slower the closer he gets, the flame bending backwards and dancing away from the candle, until he's stopped inches from his target. Then in a flash, Taniel's arm snaps back to his side, and he's back to normal. He looks at me again, utterly helpless and apologetic as I've ever seen him. My face drops as I realize what he's about to tell me.

"It's apparently against the rules."

God.

Damn.

Shit.

Mother.

Fucker.

Son of a bitch.

This is the absolute *last* thing I need right now. I've got the demon on one end of the alley, a terrified man who I'm essentially using as bait not a foot from me, and everything hinging on a Seal of Solomon that Taniel can't light in order to save innocent people all because of the freakin' "mysterious ways" the Lord wants to work in for this particular situation. Thanks for nothing, Big Guy.

Jacob, unaware of this funny little circumstance, keeps up his bravery, for all it's worth, and if I weren't distracted by everything going tits-up, I'd be proud of him. "I'm not afraid of you!"

"Uh...hey, Jacob?" I whisper. "You mind giving me a bit?"

He hisses back, "What?"

"Two seconds." I dive toward the Seal.

The demon's laugh rumbles up from deep in Alec's body. "You should be..." The laugh rolls into a screeching battle cry as Alec's fingers stretch out into those god-awful claws. I can hear the bones crack and reshape all the way down here. He shrieks again and lopes down the alley, a disjointed predator bearing down on Jacob.

There's no time: I snatch the lighter from Taniel's hands and frantically flick the thing back to life, trying to light all the candles as fast as I possibly can.

Candle One lit. The demon's bearing down fast, closing the gap to Jacob at an alarming rate.

Candle Two lit. Jacob is fighting every urge to abandon ship, and I'm starting to regret making him feel obligated to stay. I can't even be sure he'll remember the demon's true name. It was a crapshoot to begin with, and now it might cost us. If Alec turns Jacob into ribbons, I'll have put an innocent man in the line of death, and that's not something I can live with. Beyond that, the Enclave will have my ass, so that's two solid reasons to get my shit together and get these candles lit.

Like a big invisible middle finger to me, a gust of wind hits the alley and the lighter goes out. I spew curses as I give it a few frantic flicks and kick the fire back on. It's times like these I wish I were one of those mages that could shoot fire out of their hands. When this is over, I'm seeing if the Enclave has any artifacts in storage that launch fire and taking one.

Candle Three lit.

I snap my head up. "Jacob, get the hell out of here! He's getting too close!"

Jacob's standing in place, his eyes clamped shut. "No! I've almost got it!" If we all live through this, I'm buying Jacob's drinks forever. Demon-Alec is nearly on top of us, gouging the ground as he claws forward.

Candle Four lit. The lighter goes out again and flicking it won't start it up immediately. I start shaking the thing like it owes me fucking money. "Light, you stupid fucker!"

I look up again when I hear a gasp. Jacob's eyes snap open. He opens his mouth, and a baleful hiss comes out as Jacob forms what I can only imagine to be the *utukku*'s true name. Jacob's eyes roll back as the name keeps spilling out, gurgling from deep down in the throat and forcing all the air from his lungs as he recites it. Demonic languages are never pretty, but this one in particular's got that crap-your-pants kind of scary to it.

At the sound of his name, the demon-Alec skids to a stop, claws dragging along the concrete painfully. He looks like he hit a brick wall square in the face; I can see the demon trying to push forward, damn near pulling out of Alec's skin the process, but he's frozen at the sound of his name spoken against him.

I hit the lighter and it kicks on again. Candle Five lit and the circle is complete.

"You dare..." the demon croaks.

I step up behind Jacob and one-side him with my free hand. "We dare." With my other hand, I swing the Horn dagger into Alec's chest.

When the dagger connects, Alec's jaw

goes slack. Looking down, I see darkness wrapping around the blade, twisting around like inky tentacles. I give it a hard yank and peel the *utukku* from Alec Kline's mortal soul. I can barely make out the demon's true form: it's wrapped in darkness and writhing in agony from the blade's enchantment. Taniel clears the circle and I hurl the demon into the center as Alec drops to the ground, finally free of his torment.

NO.

The demon's voice billows from the center of the shadows as it twists around, trying to break free of my dagger, but Crayne's handiwork has it snared tight. Underneath the snarls, I hear a hint of desperation. It knows it's caught, and it's going to do whatever it can to break free.

NO. I WILL NOT—

"Shut up."

I take a hard swing and feel my fist connect with something soft and squishy, cutting the demon off mid-bitching. For a change of pace, everything's working. I wail into the demon, hooking in deeper with the dagger and turning the *utukku* into pulp as fast as I can. My fist beats a nice rhythm on the demon's face, or what I think is its face. It's like punching an extra-thick fog: it doesn't look like I should be connecting with anything solid, but the recoil every time tells me otherwise, so I just keep on punching until I can't hit anything anymore. The more I hit, the less of the demon remains: strands of shadow puff off with the impacts, twisting in the air inside the Seal and evaporating into nothingness. I nearly throw out my damn elbow pounding into the thing, taking out my anger for letting it get Lorelei, for letting it take over innocent people, for killing recklessly, and most of all: for ruining my goddamn vacation.

One more square hit and the shadows burst apart, dissolving into a fine mist. With a nice dramatic touch, the burst takes out the candle flames, snuffing them all in one go. The area of the Seal is darkened by the fading shadows momentarily, obscuring everything outside of it for a bit until the shadows start to fade.

"And stay down," I say to the air, hoping the bastard hears me on the way out.

TWELVE.

Lorelei glides along the surface of the water, her passage slow and light, patrolling the shores of the river for potential victims. The water ripples gently behind her, barely disturbed by her passage, only reacting to the tiny wisps of wind that spin out from her ethereal form. She floats, sad and alone, looking for some warm soul to keep her company, some warm body that she can take to the water with her.

She stops. A strange sensation rises in her chest, warm and swelling. It feels inviting, calming, enveloping. It feels...like love. Love and vengeance intertwined. It seeps through her, fills her. She knows she has been avenged, that the one who sent her to her demise has left this mortal coil.

Tears run down her cheeks, blending with the water running down from her soaking hair. She smiles, a truly genuine smile, the first one she can remember. The warmth in her chest expands, filling her body. She feels the warmth rising up inside her, radiating from within her, folding around her like a beautiful cocoon. Her smile grows brighter as her body fades away in its utter brilliance.

    The waters are calm once more.

THIRTEEN.

It's the calm after the storm, and damn it sounds sweet.

The alley's quiet again as the darkness dwindles down. I fan out my coat, kicking off what's left of the clinging shadows, watching them dance in the air before they disappear. I don't want any traces of this demonic bastard left when I leave this alley; if I have to personally scrub the walls of any funny-looking shadows, I will.

I give a look around. Taniel's standing just outside the Seal, stoic and still. Jacob is bracing himself on the alley wall, taking in what he just witnessed. Alec Kline is starting to wake up. I prioritize and move over to Jacob, helping him stand steady.

"I'm proud of you, Jacob," I say, looking him in the eyes. "Not many folks can face down something as pure evil as that the way you did. Lorelei would be proud of you, too."

Jacob forces a shaky smile. "I...I just hope she's in a better place."

I cast a look back at Taniel. He looks contemplative for a moment, then nods. "I can guarantee it," I say to Jacob.

"How do you live like this? How do you go through life seeing what you see and knowing what you know?"

I shrug. "I just gotta. It's the way things are. Would you go back, knowing what you know now?"

"Yes."

Oh. "Well...you can't. Unfortunately. So you've gotta learn to live with what you've got now. This is the truth of the matter, and now you're witness to it."

Jacob nods. "I understand."

"Good."

"Wh—what the hell's going on?"

That last bit is Alec Kline, coming to his senses and starting to realize that he is definitely not where he started this adventure. He's propped himself up on the ground, eyes wide in fear and confusion. His face is twitching, and I can tell that the memories of the past day or so are starting to bubble back to the surface. Jacob and I move over to him as it all hits him.

"My wife...where's my wife?" Alec grabs onto my coat from the ground and looks up at me desperately. "Where is my wife?? Where is—oh...oh no, no, no, God no..." Tears start streaming down his face. "Stacy," he wails, "I killed her! I killed...ohhhhh." He's moaning and starting to crack fast.

"Alec," I say, hushed. "It wasn't you. It—"

"If I may," Taniel interrupts, stepping forward. I stand to one side as Taniel kneels level to Alec. Alec looks at him, a face full of sorrow, and Taniel places a hand on his cheek, a glow of gold wrapping around them both. In the glow I see Alec begin to calm, realization and comprehension crossing his face. Turning slightly, Taniel extends a hand to Jacob.

Jacob looks to me uneasily, so I nod to give him a go-ahead and he takes Taniel's hand, the glow extending over to him as well: a small consolation for what the demon put him through. I'm almost envious of the bliss they're experiencing as Taniel gives them the closure they need, but I know that the kind of closure I'll need would take more than a moment in the holy sun, so I sit back and watch these two receive it instead. After what they've been through, they deserve it.

Alec looks up at me, then to Taniel, a few tears still running down his cheeks. "Thank you...I think I understand now..." He smiles, serene.

Taniel smiles warmly, looking to Jacob. Jacob nods in turn. I step forward to join the group. "Alec, Jacob...I think you two are going to have a lot to talk about."

Alec rises to his feet, in a state of serenity. "Thank you..." he beams and walks out of the alley the way he came. Jacob watches him walk, then turns back to me. Whatever whammy Taniel put on him quelled what was left of his fear and confusion. He looks more composed and level-headed than I've seen him since I first encountered him.

"Thank you, Talon," he says. "For everything. Can I find you if I need you?"

"I'll be right here," I nod.

Jacob smiles and follows Alec out of the alley. I watch them exit, waiting until they're clear of the alley, then I turn to Taniel. He's looking at me like he took my bike out for a spin without telling me. I know he's embarrassed at not being able to light the candles, so I try to encourage him.

"You did a good thing there, Taniel."

"It was the least I could do. I'm sorry, Talon. The rules—"

I hold up a hand. "I get it. You did what you could." I give the dagger one more look over before thrusting it back into my belt. I'll have to get this back to Crayne so she can store it in the archives with the rest of the artifacts. It'll make a nice addition: our very own demon-sticking knife. "Sucks having to play by the rules, don't it?"

"I can neither confirm nor deny that."

I smirk. "That's what I thought. Well, now that the damage is done, what say we head back inside and I finish up what's left of my vacation drinking myself stupid?"

"As you wish, Talon Pike. As you wish."

With that, I feel his hand weigh down on my shoulder and we're right back in the bar where we started. The crowd's still murmuring and drinking and kicking back. Some asshat decided to liven up the place with Joy Division. I blame the vamps.

To the center of the city where all roads meet, waiting for you
To the depths of the ocean where all hopes sank, searching for you
I was moving through the silence without motion, waiting for you
In a room with a window in the corner I found truth

My beer's still sitting in its spot. Fortunately, folks have learned not to touch my stuff. I pick it up.

"Hah! Still cold," I exclaim with pleasure. Now that's what I call a solid wrap-up to an eventful evening.

Taniel raises a glass of his own. I'm not sure what's in it, but I can bet it's not alcoholic as I know it and I can't find it anywhere on this planet without bribing some holy folks. "A toast to a job well done," he says.

I clink glasses with him. "I can drink to that." I toss back what's left of my beer and turn back to continue conversation, but Taniel's already good and gone. Damn that fucker. I laugh and shake my head.

A hand slams down on the bar top next to me, and I follow the arm all the way up to a very bewildered Catarina, with Crow by her side. "I have been looking all over for you! Where did you go?"

I push my empty bottle down the bar a bit, to get Rhys' attention. "Things happened kinda fast."

"Where is the demon," she demands. She's ready to kick ass, and I'd feel bad about letting her down if I hadn't given Jacob a chance at redemption in the process.

"Back to its hole," I answer.

"And the girl's soul?"

"We avenged her death. She's resting in the Happy Place now."

Catarina is fuming, and she looks like

she's ready to take her aggression out on me. "You were to wait for my return! Avenging the girl was my burden."

"No, it was *our* burden," I say with a point. "And moreover it was Jacob Rocca's, and now he's helped to lift his burden."

"...what?"

"I'll explain later," I say as Rhys walks over with another beer, placing it down in front of me. I'm too worn out to go into the whole thing again. Right now I want to spend the rest of the night in this bar, killing beers instead of monsters. I look over to my left and see that some poor idiot left a half a pack of cigarettes on the bar. Not my brand, but they'll do. I reach over and slip one out, popping the top on the new beer with my other hand. "And that makes us done for the day, I reckon."

Catarina still looks mad, but once I explain, she'll understand. I fire up the trusty lighter and get the first lungful of smoke I've had in ages. All in a day's work, yeah?

Crow smiles. "The industrious ant, symbolizing group effort. Though it seems it was not the group I anticipated."

"Looks like it, Crow. World's still full of surprises, huh?"

I barely get a second puff in before some asshole's hand reaches over my shoulder and plucks the cigarette from my mouth.

"Don't get too comfortable."

I know this particular asshole's voice. I know it well and it's about the last voice I want to hear right now. With a groan, I swivel on my stool to see Corbin snuffing out my cig on the heel of his boot, looking annoyingly pleased with himself.

Rhys leans on the bar and regards Corbin dryly. "Your usual, Corbin? Oh wait, that's right: you're banned from my bar. Get the fuck out."

Corbin ignores Rhys, flicking the dead cigarette away onto the floor. "None of your swill for me, Eros."

I rub my eyes, not in the mood for this. "What the hell do you want, Corbin? I just wrapped up a job—on my days off, no less. I'm on break."

"Is that what you called that mess outside? I thought Eros' boozers were just restless."

Catarina and Crow lean back on the bar, watching the spectacle. I give them a grim look before turning back to Corbin. "You gonna tell me or just bust my nuts the rest of the night?"

Corbin holds up his hands, a wicked grin sprawled across that smug little face. "No, no, you're right. I'm here on business, Talon Pike." He reaches into one of the too-many zippers on his coat and produces an envelope. He drops it in front of me, unceremoniously.

"You've been summoned."

The envelope has an uncanny weight to it. I stare at it intensely. This definitely isn't good. The envelope is yellowed, aged and brittle and sealed with an old-style wax seal, an embossed wyrm wrapped in a circle around a gothic-styled 'E.' It's not the kind of envelope I want to be getting in general, much less right now. I can guess why I'm being summoned.

Corbin keeps talking. "And given the nature of the summons, I was all too happy to deliver it myself."

I keep staring at the envelope. Great. Fucking great. I go out of my way to rid the world of a murder-crazy shadow demon and avenge the soul of a girl turned rusalka—*on my day off*—and now I have my own organization on my ass about it, with Corbin acting as their fucking mailman. What a nice little bow on this shit gift of a day.

Corbin puts a hand on the bar near me, leaning in between me and Catarina. "So say goodbye to your little playmates and let's go."

I give Corbin a hard glare. "Yeah, Corbin, let's go."

And that's how Corbin wound up face-first on the sidewalk outside of Rhys'.

I mean, can you blame me? It's still my day off, as far as I'm concerned, and watching Corbin bounce off the ground adds a little cheer back to my night. Little prick deserved it, anyway.

"You go on ahead," I tell him after he skids to a stop. "I'll catch up with you when I'm done."

Corbin picks himself up, a little blood trickling on his lip. He wipes it off on his sleeve. "I'll wait right here, Talon Pike. Right here."

"Uh-huh." I let the door swing back shut and walk back to my seat at the bar. I resume my seat, pick up my bottle, and take another long drink as I stare at the envelope.

Catarina sits next to me. "What is it, Talon?"

I sigh. "Work shit, Catarina. Just work shit."

Once I finish this off, I'm probably going to have one hell of a reaming waiting for me. The Enclave takes their assignments seriously, and me going off-book and hijacking Corbin's task, regardless of results, breaks their idea of an ordered system. Given that the group thrives on order in the chaos, that doesn't bode so well for me.

Lorelei flashes through my head briefly, and I imagine her released and happy again.

Hell with it. They can tear me a new one all they like. I know what I did was right. I finish my drink and wave down Rhys for another with

extras for Catarina and Crow. I've still got a bit
before I absolutely have to be there. Let 'em wait
a little. I've earned a break.

   After all, it's still my day off.

ACKNOWLEDGEMENTS

<u>Zachary Vaudo</u>

First things first: my love and thanks to my parents, Damian and Jill, and my loves, Ellie Collins and Nikki A Eva (who make awesome stuff of their own, by the way!), for supporting me and encouraging me, both in this and beyond. I couldn't do any of this without you. Extra-special thanks to Ellie for helping me lay this whole monster out and make it pretty and professional for you all.

Notable thanks to Lex Lewis, AKA Talon Pike himself. That's his lovely mug on the cover, and his voice you're hearing in your head (probably). Without him, this doesn't exist.

Special thanks to everyone else involved in the Talon project: David Haddad, Lizabeth Jayne Smith, Kelly Frances Hager, Susan Bowie, Keith

Bobby Creech, for helping me fine-tune some of Talon's talents.

<u>Rebecca Eagle Lewis</u>

I want to thank my influences: My grandmother Stella Eagle. My father Joe Eagle, mother Debbie Mulinax. My son Harley Eagle. Alex Lewis. And Raven Hart.

Featured Songs:

p. 22: "Neverland" – The Damned, *Grave Disorder* (2001), Nitro Records

p. 25, 26, 28: "The Humbling River" – Puscifer, *Sound into Blood and Wine* (2010), Puscifer Entertainment

p. 81: "Burning in the Undertow of God" – The Angelic Process, *Weighing Souls with Sand* (2007), Profound Lore Records

p. 96: "Shadowplay" – Joy Division, *Unknown Pleasures* (1979), Factory Records

Brooks, John Prew, Jo Veitenheimer, Larry Bowie, Secret Harris, Trevor Garner, Richard Hampton, Chris Booth, TJ Garland, Julia Stahl, Michelle Alderman, Lauren Hope Williams, Bowen Cheek, Paul Steenhoek, Oliver Kasiske, Shana Melton, Raven Hart, and so many more (some we haven't even met yet!). This is a crazy expanding universe we're building, and all the hands involved help it grow. You're the creative life-blood. You're the magic. OK, that part sounds cheesy, but seriously: thanks, for all of it.

All the thanks to Jennifer Adams, K. Anduze, and Erika A. Pratte for scouring this text and making sure I didn't muck the whole thing up.

Thank you to my aunt, Karen Davis, for her support, both emotional and financial—I couldn't have put this out without your help!

And thanks to mystic adviser

ABOUT THE AUTHORS

Zachary Vaudo is a writer, filmmaker, and musician based in Atlanta. He enjoys long walks on the beach, comic books, and delving into the dark recesses of the human mind. Zak is the writer of *Stan the Zombie* and writer/executive producer of Atlanta's *Uncanny X-Men* fan series. He's done some other stuff, too, but after the rest of the book you're probably tired of reading all his words by this point.

Rebecca Eagle Lewis is a some-time writer, full-time mom from Lithia Springs. Her favorite things include coffee, reading, and her fur-babies: Chewey, Iggy Pup, and Puppycat.